Sticks and Stones
and Skeleton Bones

JAMIE GILSON

Sticks and Stones and Skeleton Bones

Illustrated by Dee deRosa

Lothrop, Lee & Shepard Books
New York

With special thanks to the Peace-makers at Mitchell Elementary-Middle School in Racine, Wisconsin, and the Conflict Managers at the Sunrise Drive Elementary School in Tucson, Arizona.

Copyright © 1991 by Jamie Gilson
All rights reserved. No part of this book may be reproduced or utilized in any form or by any means, electronic or mechanical, including photocopying and recording, or by any information storage and retrieval system, without permission in writing from the Publisher. Inquiries should be addressed to Lothrop, Lee & Shepard Books, a division of William Morrow & Company, Inc., 105 Madison Avenue, New York, New York 10016
Printed in the United States of America
First Edition 1 2 3 4 5 6 7 8 9 10
Library of Congress Cataloging in Publication Data
Gilson, Jamie. Sticks and stones and skeleton bones / by Jamie Gilson ; illustrated by Dee deRosa
p.   cm. Summary : Hobie, whose fifth grade class is meeting in a shopping mall because the school was devastated by a flood, has a disagreement with his best friend Nick that escalates into a big fight as the day continues.
ISBN 0-688-10098-8
[1. Friendship—Fiction. 2. Schools—Fiction. 3. Shopping malls—Fiction.]   I. DeRosa, Dee, ill.   II. Title. PZ7.G4385St 1991   [Fic]—dc20
90-49610 CIP AC

For Suzanne Miller
and
George Furth

Contents

Sticks and Stones
and Skeleton Bones

1. The Muds of Time

Nick Rossi pointed the flashlight in my face. "My fingers are practically Popsicles," he said. "My toes are so cold I can't feel them. Let's get out of here." He aimed the light back at the hole I was digging. "Come on, Hobie. I just saw Frosty the Snowman thumbing a ride to Florida. What could you *possibly* need to dig up on a night like this?"

I leaned on the garden trowel and peeled off another inch of dirt. The hole I was digging was exactly five footsteps from the big maple tree next to my backyard fence, just like the map said. And the map was right. I knew it was right because I'd drawn it myself. The ground against my knees was oozy, even though snow was falling fast. The wind was whipping in one ear and out the other.

"It's a secret," I told him, which was weird because I hardly ever keep secrets from Nick. "But you can guess, if you want to."

First Nick shivered, then he sighed. "Okay. It's . . . gold coins," he guessed. "Gold coins from the time when the Romans fought lions in Illinois. And they're so rare they'll make us rich and famous and we won't have to take the test tomorrow, which we haven't studied for because we're doing this. Right?"

I looked up and shook my head. "Wrong. Too bad."

Nick shifted his feet and tucked his free hand into his armpit. "I know. You're digging out an ancient underground microwave oven. It's got this huge mug of cocoa in it with four inches of marshmallows on top. And we'll zap it to make the marshmallows soft and the cocoa hot enough to burn your tongue. Right?"

"How'd you guess?" I put the trowel down. "No kidding, you're really going to like this. I just completely forgot it was out here. I mean, what with school and the high water and all." Nick and I started fifth grade in September and *that* was crazy enough. But then almost

2

right away, in October, the Hawk River went bananas and flooded out our houses and streets and school, and everything turned totally bizarre. So, this fall wasn't just your basic orange leaves and trick or treat.

"I hate to mention this, but whatever you've got in there, if it was buried before the flood," Nick said, aiming the light at the hole, "by now it smells like rotten river carp." He shifted the light to his other hand. "Hey, listen, Hobie, I gotta get home."

It's true the river left some fish behind. We learned at school how the Pilgrims buried fish with their corn to make it grow. Well, for a long time our yards smelled like Jack was trying to grow a cornstalk bigger than his beanstalk.

"Okay, you don't have to stay," I told him, scooping faster. The snow swirled around my ears. Nick lives next door, so he could get home in two seconds, but I was pretty sure he wouldn't go.

He flicked the light off. "I hear something."

"Duck," I whispered. He ducked. I crouched low over the hole to hide what I was doing. All I could hear was our breathing. Then, from behind the fence that separates our yards, there came a kind of scurry. "Squirrel," I hissed, but waited low. Nothing. The only sound was snow turning to hail and dropping like BBs.

From a bush on the other side of the fence a flashlight poked out about three feet away and zigzagged us up and down. "Gotcha," the voice behind it said. Then it began to cackle. *He* began to cackle.

He was Nick's little brother, Toby, who is going through the terrible fours. He also went through the terrible ones, twos, and threes.

Toby was giggling like somebody had just told him a joke about underwear. He thinks underwear jokes are very funny. "What you doing?" he asked. "Mom says come in." He pressed his face against the wire fence. I bet his mother didn't even know he was outside, because all he had on under his open jacket was a pair of Batman pajamas.

"Arrrrrrrrgg," Nick growled. He flicked the light on and tucked it under his chin so he looked deep-shadowed like a big-time neck-biting vampire. "Vee are hunting, leetle von. Vee are searching," he said, in a true Transylvanian accent, "for vild verevolves for our vild verevolf zoo."

4

For a second or two Toby was silent. "Ni-ick! Mom *said.*" Toby doesn't scare all that easy. "What you doing? What you doing in the dark? I'm coming over."

I didn't want him over. I sure didn't want him to see what I'd been digging. Something oozed out of the earth and wiggled past my little finger, something slimy. I sucked my breath in, but then I smiled, wrapped my hand gently around the wiggler, and said, "Caught one." I was quiet, but loud enough for Toby to hear.

"Really?" Toby whispered. "You caught a werewolf? Right now?"

"Just a baby." I stood up and moved toward him. "I don't think it's got its teeth yet," I told him. "You want it?" Toby stepped back. "Come on, hold out your hand."

Toby cupped his hands next to the fence and I let the long, fat night crawler slither into his fingers.

He took it and swallowed most of his yelp.

"Now go back inside quick and put it some-place dark," I told him, "but don't look at it and don't let any light shine on it or it'll turn into something really ordinary and dumb."

"My very own baby werewolf. Thank you,

Hobie," he said proudly, heading toward home. "Mom is going to be mad at you," he called over his shoulder to Nick.

Turning back to me, Nick stuck the light under his nose and raised his eyebrows. "You got a big supply of werewolves there?"

"It was just a worm," I told him. "But I didn't want Toby to see."

"See what?" he asked.

"The stuff I'm really digging up. I'm not *supposed* to dig it up till 2013."

"Twenty thirteen what?"

"The *year* 2013, that's what." I went back to tossing dirt.

"Is this a joke?" he asked me. "I know it isn't April first by the snowdrifts building up behind my ears. It's November twenty-first and I'm out of here." He turned to go.

"One second . . ." I could hardly keep from laughing as I pushed the last of the mushy earth aside, reached in, and pulled out what I'd been aiming for—a mud-caked, slimy, black plastic bag, tied at the top with a hard knot. Every night since the middle of July, night crawlers had been sliding down its slippery sides. This was going to be *so* funny.

"And heeeere's treasure!" I raised the bag

high and waved it in front of him. Hunks of mud slid from it onto the snow.

He shone the light on me and the grungy bag. "You don't want my baby brother to see *that*?" he asked. "Look, Toby's big on dirt. Very big. I've seen him sun-bake brownies made of it, eat them, and lick his lips. He *collects* dirty words," Nick went on. "I don't, somehow, think a muddy sack would ruin his day."

The hail began to ping down faster, pea-sized.

Nick's back-porch light flashed on.

"Hey, what are you boys doing out there?" his dad shouted. "It's snowing. It's getting late. And it's a Monday night. School tomorrow. What's going on?"

"Nothing," Nick called back.

I held the bag behind my back. "We're working on a school project, Mr. Rossi," I yelled. "But we're almost finished."

"Well . . ." There was a long pause. "All right, but hurry it up," he said, and went back in to watch TV.

"Is this really for class?" Nick asked me. "You're not digging up old gerbil bones, are you? Is this where we buried Frisky and Gumball?"

We were studying bones at school, but I wasn't about to dig Frisky and Gumball up for their bones. You can get bones from fried chicken. "Of course not." I kept my voice low. "I just said that. Parents never make you stop school stuff, even in the dark."

The knot was too tight, so I just tore open the yucky plastic bag and dropped it on the ground. Then I pulled out the cracker tin and soaked poster board that were inside and tucked them both under my jacket. My belly looked like I lived on double-creme Oreos. "You're not going to believe what's in here," I told Nick.

He followed me into my house and through the kitchen, where Mom and Dad sat drinking coffee, eating the rest of the blueberry pie, and watching TV. Two guys were carting somebody off the field on Monday-night football. We didn't stop to watch, but hurried on down the hall, up the steps, and into my room.

I slammed my bedroom door and leaned against it. I could hardly keep a straight face. This was going to be a blast. Nick and I were going to laugh all night about this. All week. All year. If only I could keep from cracking up before I got to the punch line.

8

First I kicked aside my math and science homework, a stack of old magazines, and yesterday's socks and underwear, and then we sat down in the middle of my fuzzy green rug.

"After this we've got to study," Nick said. "Miss Ivanovitch told us we had to know our bones from waist to toe for the test tomorrow, and I don't."

"As soon as we're done," I promised. "But you're gonna love this."

I whipped the soggy poster board out of my jacket and handed it to Nick. Practically every letter was crying, but you could still make out the message.

He held it up to the light. "This is a mess." But then, squinching his eyes, he began to read out loud. *"Beware. If anybody opens this time capsule before July 4, 2013, their ears will turn to prunes, their noses to bill . . ."*

"Dill. Dill pickles."

". . . pickles, their eyes to little peeled onions, and their belly buttons to . . ." what's that?" He pointed.

"To Gob Stoppers," I explained, laughing. I mean, this was hysterical.

". . . to Gob Stoppers." And he went on like he didn't understand it was funny. *"This is*

no lie, so beware." He gave me a weird look. "If this is no lie, Hobie Hanson, you should start looking like a grocery store any minute. So, how did this treasure get into your backyard?"

Actually, that was one question I didn't want to answer. I shrugged. "A bunch of us buried it last summer while you were away at Mighty Byte Computer Camp."

"A bunch of us?"

"Oh, you know. Toby was here. That's why I had to get rid of him. So he wouldn't tell Molly and Lisa and Michelle and Jenny."

"*Girls?* You buried this can in your backyard with a bunch of *girls*?"

"Oh, come *on.* R.X. was here, too. And Trevor. Toby put in a Go-Bot with a loose head. Some other kid put in a dinosaur. The reason I don't want them to know is we all agreed we wouldn't dig it up. We buried it for the future," I said, seriously. "For our children. And our children's children." I pried open the cracker tin and took out a coffee can wrapped with red tape. It looked pretty dry.

"Wait a minute," Nick said. "You mean I stood out there in the dark catching double pneumonia to keep my little brother from telling your children's children you dug up his broken robot? Wouldn't it have been a whole lot easier just to leave it stuck in the mud?"

I tore the tape from the coffee can. "Well, maybe, but before the ground froze I just wanted to check and see if the stuff lived through the flood. And I wanted to *show* you. I'm going to bury it all back tomorrow night."

"So Molly and Lisa won't find out?" he asked, grinning.

I flipped the lid off and dumped everything out. "Don't even *think* about it." Besides the loose-headed Go-Bot and a slightly chewed dinosaur, there was a green butterfly hair clip that one of the girls had put in, a few folded paper stars, a pair of glow-in-the-dark shoelaces, and like that.

Nick looked at me as if I was bonkers. "That's it? Well, wow, I guess," he said, like that was that. Then he reached over and grabbed the picture of a skeleton that was sticking out of my notebook. "Okay, moving right along, folks, where do you fall when you fall on your coccyx?"

"The bones can wait one minute more," I told him. This wasn't going exactly the way I'd planned. Somehow the stuff I dug up had seemed a whole lot better when we buried it. I tried again, picking up a blue plastic soap box that I'd wrapped tight with tape. "You've got to see *this*. Inside this ordinary soap box— you're not going to believe it—set in Silly Putty, is almost my entire set of baby teeth." I rocked over on my back laughing. "It looks *very* funny."

"You're going to look even funnier tomorrow with a Gob Stopper for a belly button," he said, "but I promise I won't point it out to more than four or five girls." He checked the bone sheet again. "Okay, which is thicker, the femur or the fibula?"

"Wait, wait, just one second more," I told him. "Here's something I promise you'll like. No kidding."

Nick still wasn't getting excited. Maybe it was because we'd buried the stuff when he wasn't here.

I quick picked up a can that said peanut brittle on it and handed it to him. "Take a look," I said. "Molly put it in, and it's the best. She said it's to help those future guys understand our taste."

Sometimes Nick likes Molly, so I knew he'd be interested. This was going to be *so* funny.

It was one of those trick cans you get in magic stores that looks like it's got candied peanuts inside, but really it's this coiled-up spring snake. Nick would unscrew it, the snake would jet-tail it out of there, and it would scare the hiccups out of him for the rest of his life. Then he'd laugh like crazy.

"Molly found it in the park." I kept talking to keep him from thinking about what he was going to do. "After that we'll study," I said with my straightest face, so as not to give it away.

He turned the lid with a jerk and, as he screwed the cap off, leaned forward to see what was inside.

Zappo!

Four months underground hadn't killed it, hadn't even tamed it. The snake inside snapped out like a high pop fly. It flew fast and free and caught him square in the nose.

I laughed. That was just what it was supposed to do.

And even funnier, the wire spring had, somehow, slipped out of its thin plastic snakey-looking jacket and hooked itself onto the inside of his nostril. It hung on. Nick had a snake dangling out of his nose. He looked really wild, like Nick with an elephant's trunk.

He was Babar. He was Dumbo. I grabbed my sides laughing. I rolled on the floor.

I would have *kept* laughing, too, and he would have started, I know he would, but that's when he did this dumb thing that began it all. Instead of just letting the stupid snake hang there and look weird, he tried to yank it away. He grabbed the slippery plastic sides and pulled straight down. He shouldn't have done that because, when he pulled, the loose wire stuck into his nose. It hooked him like a fish. Blood began to drip onto the rug.

Nick couldn't even see what he'd done. He didn't know he looked like a trout. When I reached out to help, he tried to bat my hand away. But I forced my fingers right up there anyway, and as carefully as I could with him yelling and dodging, I unthreaded the snake. His nose had a hole he could wear a ruby in if he was a rock star or a rich prince. There wasn't a ruby in the hole, though; there was more blood. I grabbed yesterday's heap of laundry from the floor and jammed it over his face to stop the flow.

Nick pressed a finger against his nose like you do when you have a regular nosebleed. And I don't think it was till he picked up the peanut-brittle can for the second time that he realized what he'd fallen for.

That's when he threw a red-streaked T-shirt at me.

"I'm sorry. I just wanted you to see the stuff we . . ." I tried to explain. "I was just trying to be funny."

"I'm not laughing," he said, pressing the back of his hand against his nose. "I'm bleeding. I don't even know why I fell for that. It's an old trick. And you know what's going to happen? I'm going to get home and my dad's going to think you beat me up and my mom's going to ask me if we finished our homework and Toby's going to want to show me his genuine werewolf. I'm not laughing at all."

He stalked out of my room. The coffee can rolled into a corner. Soon the front door crashed shut.

"Hobie?" Mom called. "What's wrong with Nick?"

16

2. You're Going to Get It

Nick wasn't on the bus the next morning. His mom must have taken him. He was already at school when I got there. Not *really* school. We don't go to a real school. I mean, we used to. But when Central School, where we've gone since kindergarten, got washed out in the big flood, the first floor was totaled. They hauled our second-floor desks and some chalkboards and other unwet stuff over to this closed-up store, Bob's Togs for All the Family, in the Wilhurst Mall. We go to school in a mall. It's pretty weird. We've got to study in this huge space that has escalators and counters, and we go to gym in the women's dress department and get clarinet lessons in the freight elevator. You never really quite get used to it.

As soon as I got off the bus in the mall parking lot, I spotted Nick's red and white striped cap. He was up on the Bob's Togs loading dock, where the school's front door is located. It looked like he was talking to Robert "Bob" Bobb himself, the guy who owned the store when it was one. He'd been there on our first day and we'd all written him Friendly Letters to thank him for letting us use the space.

"Hey, Nick," I yelled, waving both my arms. I was about to go tell him I didn't study for the bone test because I couldn't figure out if your wrist bones are above your waist or below it, but Trevor and R.X. got to me first.

Trevor grabbed me by the arm. "Boy, is Nick ever mad at you!" he said.

"Me?"

"You. And you better be plenty careful. Have you seen his nose?" R.X. asked.

"Well, last night it was just a little . . ."

"It may have been little last night, but this morning it looks like a light bulb," Trevor said.

"I called him Rudolf," R.X. went on. And he went on laughing, too.

"That's nothing," Trevor said. "Rolf called him Fat Snout. I called him Beet Beak. He said it was your fault and that he was going to get you."

"His mom made him come to school."

"He didn't want to," Trevor said.

"I don't blame him, either. He looks like Bozo. He's going to get you, for sure. He said you stink."

"His mom said he might have to get a shot for rabies."

"Rabies?" I didn't understand this at all. "That snake didn't have rabies," I told them.

"Snake?"

"What snake?" R.X. asked, and he and Trevor looked at each other funny. "Anyway, I don't think he said rabies. I think he said he might have to get a shot for lockjaw."

"Lockjaw? I didn't lock his jaws. I didn't *touch* him. I didn't lay a pinkie on him. He's a liar if he said I did. I don't think he . . ."

The first bell rang and when I turned around, Nick had already gone inside. He hadn't told on me, though. He hadn't told R.X. and Trevor I'd dug up the time capsule we'd buried, or they'd have said that, too. They'd have known about the snake can. And they'd have been mad. Old Nick, he was okay. He wasn't really mad at me. I knew he wasn't.

I hurried inside, where kids were still yelling. The second bell was ten minutes away. Thanksgiving was coming up, and some girl in a long apron passed me carrying a papier-mâché turkey under her arm.

I headed for the washroom, but the line went on forever. Washroom lines are always long at Bob's Togs. The place was built for shoppers, not for two-hundred-some kids who drink tons of orange juice and milk for breakfast. I cut in front of Eugene, this kid in my class.

"I bet you're going to the john to hide out," he leaned forward and whispered in my ear.

"What do you mean hide out? They practically time you in there," I told him. "Anyway, why would I want to hide?"

Eugene grinned. "Everybody says Nick is out to get you." He looked me over like he was trying to decide how much I weighed. "I personally am not sure Nick could beat you up, but if he's mad enough, I bet he could make your nose even bigger and redder than his. I don't know. What do you think?" And he grinned again like this was some joke.

The bell rang and the line dissolved as

everybody scrambled to their classes. Miss Ivanovitch, our teacher, lets us go back to the john if we were in line, but we have to get to the room in time for attendance and milk count. Actually, we don't have rooms. In the store, classes are separated by chalkboards and shelves and stuff.

Nick was already sitting in the front row, right where I came in. My desk is in the back. Miss Ivanovitch had separated us because we'd flicked a pile of spitballs at each other one day while Trevor was giving a boring talk on toenails and how they grow.

"How you doing?" I asked Nick as I passed, but he kept his eyes on his skeleton sheet, boning up. Still, I could see his nose was swollen and kind of shiny. He didn't look like Bozo, exactly, but he did look weird.

As I walked down the aisle to my desk I could feel people staring at me. Molly Bosco rolled her eyes when I passed.

I felt like saying it wasn't my fault, so I took two steps back and said to her, "Listen, I didn't *do* anything, so don't look at me like that."

"Right," she said, like she knew better.

Miss Ivanovitch shushed the class and we stood and pledged to the flag.

I sank into my seat.

"Well, since Thanksgiving is Thursday," Miss Ivanovitch began brightly, "we only have a three-day week, so let's turn everything up to fast forward. In social studies we have to get the Pilgrims from midocean to their big feast. In science, we must polish off the skeleton from cranium to phalanges. And there's more." She smiled. "Much more."

"Ho-ho-ho!" we heard suddenly from somewhere outside our class. "Ho-ho-ho," a huge belly laugh. It was much more, all right.

Jingle jingle jingle. "Ho-ho-ho." All this clatter was coming from the escalator in the middle of the store. The escalators are shut off, so sometimes our principal, Miss Hutter, stands halfway up one to make announcements. Miss Hutter was there, but she wasn't making the *jingle*-ho's. Santa Claus was doing that.

No kidding. Santa Claus. This bearded fat guy dressed up in a red suit clamped with a shiny black belt was waving to kids on both sides of the escalator, his stocking cap bobbing, his cheeks pinker than Nick's nose and twice as puffy.

Miss Hutter was holding the bullhorn. "People," her voice blasted. "People. May I have your attention, please, people. I have a delightful surprise for you. I'd like you to welcome this jolly old elf who has come to visit us from his igloo in the Wilhurst Mall."

The jolly old elf held onto his belly, nodded his head, and swayed from side to side like the Santas in store windows. We laughed when we saw him, in spite of ourselves.

"Hello there, boys and girls," Santa Claus called out. And even though we were all fourth, fifth, and sixth graders who weren't going to be sitting on his knee asking for Mack Avengers or Creepy Crawlers, most kids called back, "Hello, Santa Claus."

"Ho-ho-ho," he sang out again, loud and clear over the bullhorn. His huge laugh sounded just right for a guy who paints toy clowns for a living. "Well, boys and girls," he went on, "I do have a special message. I've come down from the North Pole early to tell you that I've been watching and that I know you've been good little girls and boys. And I'm here to announce that for your fine behavior, for not entering the mall proper during school hours, and for being courteous in the mall parking lot, your school will receive a special thank-you present."

Miss Hutter and a few kids over on the sixth-grade side of the escalator clapped. Santa Claus bobbed his head at them.

Molly Bosco, three seats up from me, gave a note to Lisa Soloman, who sits behind her. I watched as Lisa read it, turned, made an ape face at me, and then handed the note back to Eugene. He read it, folded it up, and tossed it on my desk. Miss Ivanovitch looked straight at me, so I smiled at her and crossed my arms over the note.

"Your principal, Miss Hutter, suggested what the present might be, and the elves and I thought her suggestion was . . . very modern." Santa Claus rested the bullhorn on his mountainous belly. The fat was fake, I decided, either pillows or a life-preserver vest. "The science elves," he went on, "are still working on the presents you are to receive for your good guest behavior. They'll be delivered to your old school when you return there this February. What do you think they'll be?"

I didn't know what to think they'd be.

Chemistry sets? Probably not. Rulers? Not very modern. Automatic paper towel dispensers?

"Because of your fine behavior in the mall," he went on, "your school will receive—straight from the North Pole—eight brand-spanking-new . . . computers. What do you think of that?"

Computers. *Eight* computers. All of us sucked in our breath at once. We knew what to think. I mean, that wasn't candy canes. It was like winning the whole Wheel of Fortune. Central School had only owned three computers in the first place, and those were old. Besides, they'd been gargled up in the flood.

"So, boys and girls, those gifts will serve to remind you of the well-behaved weeks you have spent and are going to spend right here in the beautiful Wilhurst Mall."

This time there was big-time clapping, shouting, stamping of feet, and whistling, too, from both sides of the escalator.

"As you may know, today is the beginning of the holiday season here in the mall," the Santa Claus guy went on. "The decorations are up and the lights are lit. It's my first day in the brand-new North Pole igloo. So, when you're shopping with your family, stop in to see me and my favorite nephew, Oscar Claus."

He swept his right arm from behind him and raised it high. But your basic five-finger hand wasn't at the end of his arm. Instead, he had a big-mouthed, red-haired, red-suited puppet.

"Hi there, boys and girls," a completely different voice called. It sounded a lot like a cartoon squirrel. "Unc and I sure will be glaaaaad to see you. You keep on being goood little boys and girls, now, you hear?"

But then the puppet began to cough. All the kids who'd stopped listening and started talking got quiet again because this puppet was really hacking away. And just when I thought Miss Hutter would have to hug Santa Claus in a major Heimlich maneuver, he said to the puppet, sounding perfectly normal, "Oscar, Oscar, are you choking?"

"No," Oscar answered in his chirpy voice, "I'm not choking, I'm serious."

We all groaned. I think even Miss Hutter did.

"You are splendid children, outstanding young people," he called. "Happy snowfall to all, and to all a goooood day." He handed the bullhorn over to Miss Hutter, and laying a fin-

ger aside of his nose with a *jingle, jangle, jingle,* up the escalator he rose. Then even without hitching up Dasher, Dancer, Prancer, and Vixen, he disappeared from view. Probably he'd walked out the second-floor door into the upper level of the mall. We all clapped again. He liked us. We liked him.

"I never saw a Santa with a puppet before," Lisa said.

"Computers!" Eugene turned to me. "He promised us computers. That's big bucks. I don't know, though, sounds like a bribe to be good."

"You suppose," Marshall asked him, "if we escape into the mall and buy cookies, there'll be no green screens in our future?"

"I think," Eugene told him, "that if we sneak out and ask Santa Claus for Nintendo, Oscar will turn us in." He shook his head. "Eight computers, though, that would really be something."

"Oh, my dears, new computers," Miss Ivanovitch said. "Do you know what that means? You could rewrite your wonderful stories without agony. We could publish. You could do a really slick weekly newspaper." She sat down and began to write on a long yellow pad.

I flipped Molly's note over. On the outside, she'd written "HOBIE," with no little heart dotting the i like she usually makes. This note was to me! Those other kids had been reading *my* note. It was written in black ink, though, not in red, like she usually does.

I unfolded it slowly, as though I didn't care what was inside. "Hobie," it said, "I used to like you, but now I don't. You're the one who should have gotten the gross nose. Molly."

Okay. That did it. I couldn't trust Nick anymore. He'd told Molly I dug up the time capsule after I'd warned him I didn't want her to know. When I looked up, I could see she'd watched me read it. So had Lisa and Eugene. I shrugged, like I didn't care, like "So?"

"After art class," Miss Ivanovitch was saying, "we'll have our short bone quiz."

I mean, I *didn't* care. Molly wasn't my girl friend or anything. The note didn't make all that much difference to me. Not really.

"A *shord* bode quiz?" Nick asked. Not only did his nose look funny, but he sounded funny, too, like he had a code in his doze. "Sub of the leg bodes are *log,*" he went on, and kids laughed.

"Short quiz, Nick, not short bones," she told him, grinning. "Though that's not a bad idea. Tomorrow I'll ask you where the three smallest bones are."

"Do we have to go, like, outside after lunch?" Lisa asked. "I mean, it's really cold and gross."

"It's a winter wonderland," Miss Ivanovitch told her. "How could you want to miss it? I feel sure today's an Out Day, but Miss Hutter will make the announcement later."

She glanced at the calendar on her desk. "Amber and Marshall will be staying in. Today is the last mediator training session. We'll be meeting in Infants' Wear at noon. I hope you haven't forgotten." Marshall and Amber shook their heads. "I have presents for everyone in the mediation group," she said.

Miss Ivanovitch had been running this special class almost every day for a month, teaching two kids from each room how to mediate. I wasn't in it, so I didn't know for sure what they did. The time she told us I must have been thinking about something else. If it had to do with media, they'd be putting out a newspaper or something, which I knew Miss

Ivanovitch wanted to do. But the kids in it said it was about arguments. Mediators might be like gladiators. I remembered what they did. They argued. They also speared people from horse-drawn chariots. But I knew for sure there weren't any horses in Infants' Wear. Or spears. Maybe she'd taught them karate and the presents were bricks to break with their bare hands.

I glanced up. From the front row, Nick was staring at me, his nose like a pickled beet. Eugene saw him looking. He turned around and whispered, "Hobie Hanson, I wouldn't be you for anything in the world."

3. What's So Funny?

If we dyed Lisa's hair purple, would that be art?" Molly had a jar of blue tempera paint in one hand and a jar of red in the other. "What do you think, Mr. Sciarra?" she asked our art teacher.

Lisa, who was supposed to get mad, didn't. "I've been thinking about a change," she said, pulling her hair straight up and staring in a mirror. Art class is in the beauty shop at Bob's Togs, so the walls are lined with mirrors. "We could tip it green."

"Well, 'Art is long,' the poet says, and Lisa's hair is short," Mr. Sciarra told them. "Dying it purple or even green wouldn't change that. So, I give your idea two thumbs down."

What he meant was, don't you *dare*. He doesn't even let us paint our faces. He does let us do messier projects than we did at Central. That's because washing up is so easy here. There are six sinks, every one of them with little built-in U's where people's necks fit when they used to get their hair washed and dyed. The chairs were unscrewed and carried away, but the sinks got left behind.

Mr. Sciarra, who travels around to four schools in the district, likes teaching at Bob's best. He told us so. He also told us that some guys are going to tear down the inside walls after we go and turn the place into lots of little shops. So he's promised us that before we leave we can paint dragon murals on the art room walls. They're all Pepto-Bismol pink now, with silver feathers and green flowers splashed with shampoo and specks of hair dye. My dragon will be black and orange.

Anyway, the whole class was standing around this chairless beauty shop on the second floor, waiting to do art. Mr. Sciarra called us over to a wide counter where twenty-some slabs of clay were sitting on squares of waxed paper.

"Okay, troops," he said. "I want each of you

to take a piece of this first-rate earth. Since we made tiles last week, you know how to knead the bubbles out. After you do that, I want you to fool around with the clay until you discover something amazing inside it." He picked up two chunks and began to juggle them. "You might find a fire hydrant, or an octopus. Who's to know? If you like what you've made well enough, you can let it dry and bisque it. I'll take it over to the high school and fire it in the kiln. It's the only kiln in the district that's alive after the flood, so I can only fire a few pieces. Sorry." He tossed the clay high, almost to the ceiling, caught both chunks behind his back, and set them down on the counter.

"I want to make something flat," Molly said.

"Okay, there's a rolling pin or two up here." He held one out, along with a fat plastic sack. "This bag has various cookie cutters in it that will stamp out elephants, dinosaurs, stars, hearts, the Statue of Liberty, or even the state of Texas, if that's in your game plan. There's a meat tenderizer with which you can pound in texture, and even a garlic press in case you want to squeeze out some snakes for a jungle scene."

I grabbed one of the rolling pins and tucked it under my arm.

"Remember to score pieces you want to stick together and slather them with slip," he said. Slip is this kind of liquid clay that acts like glue. I grabbed a paper cup of it. Then I picked up a glob of clay stuck to a sheet of paper, which I put on the pink tile floor. There aren't any tables in the art room, either, but there's plenty of space, so you can stretch out on your belly if you want to.

Actually, I didn't feel much like messing with wet dirt. Last night's muck had got me in enough trouble. Not only was Nick mad, but Mom said that come spring I'd be farming po-tatoes in my mud-caked green rug. She didn't smile when she said it.

Still, I dug a few hills and valleys with my knuckles and I squeezed the clay until it oozed through my fingers. Then I rolled it into a ball, which I poked with seven pencil-hole eyes and a snout nose. After pinching on some Mickey Mouse ears, I wadded the stuff all up again and flattened it with the rolling pin. What came out was sort of round, but I still didn't know what it *was*. Maybe I'd discovered the wheel. Or a smashed smiley face. Or an orange run over by a truck.

A fly landed on my ear. At least it felt like a fly. Or a mosquito. I swatted it. Then another one hit. I hit it back. It wasn't a fly. It was clay as big as a wad of bubble gum. While I was looking at it, a third one slapped the back of my neck. It stung.

Nick was shooting them. I was sure. I'd seen him sit down behind me and cross his legs Indian style. He must have found baby cannonballs inside his clay. I wasn't going to let it bug me.

Picking up one of the globs he'd shot me with, I squashed it between my fingers. It looked like a deformed mushroom, so I cut fine tick-tack-toe lines on it and on the circle, dunked it with slip and stuck it on. Then I peeled another glob off the back of my neck. The kids behind me giggled, but I just pressed an end of it together so it looked like a mushroom, too. I glued it to the circle. The next one was bigger. I flattened it with the rolling pin. Pepperoni. Clearly I'd made thin-sliced

pepperoni. I prepared it carefully and cen-
tered it on my circle.

Plop. One more direct hit. A still bigger blob.
I could hear more laughing behind me while
I squashed that one in the garlic press and
pushed down. Out oozed bushy strands of
beard. Or it might have been a worm conven-
tion or . . . Actually, I knew what it was. It
was grated cheese. It was mozzarella cheese.
I dipped it in slip, heaped it on my circle, and
pressed down. I was on a roll.

Mr. Sciarra would *have* to bake this one. It
was pizza, the most astonishing pizza ever.
Without looking back at Nick taking glob shots
at me, I rushed to the counter to get one more
hunk of clay. The only cutter left was the one
shaped like Texas.

After rolling out a batch of pepperoni circles,
I cut three Texas pieces and placed them just
right. I figured they could be state-shaped red
peppers. I mean, why not? Mr. Sciarra was always telling us to be creative. Then I squeezed
out mounds and mounds of cheese and shaped
more mushrooms with little caps. I thought
about putting some weird stuff on it, too, like
black beetles, but in the end I decided just to

make a plain old ordinary Texas-shaped pepper, pepperoni, and mushroom pizza. When I finished, I smiled. It was awesome.

A lot of times my art projects look like garbage, but this was excellent. When it was fired it would be fantastic. It looked like you could eat it cold for breakfast.

Amber Murnyak asked for my rolling pin because she wanted to roll out a rug. I decided I could turn in the cookie cutter and garlic press, too, so I took them to the counter, where Mr. Sciarra was trying to help a kid make up her mind what to build.

When the kid finished deciding that fried eggs would work but a snowperson wouldn't, I asked Mr. S. if he'd like to see what I'd made. I mean, my pizza was going to knock his eyes out. He's always nice about it, but usually he doesn't find a whole lot to say about my stuff. "That's an interesting concept" is about as far as he goes. After I explain what I was trying to do, he says "Hmmmmmmm."

He followed me. "Hobie," he was saying, "I always suspected that clay might be your medium." And then we stopped at my spot on the floor.

I wasn't even sure it was the right spot. My

pizza wasn't pizza anymore. You couldn't tell it ever had been. While I was waiting at the counter, somebody had gotten up and stepped square in the middle of my amazing pie, so that the heaps of cheese were squashed, the mushrooms were blobs again, and the Texas-shaped peppers had merged with the thin-rolled pepperoni. It was a footprint in a circle surrounded by junk. That's all it was.

The kids around me were breaking up. They'd seen who did it. I hadn't seen, but I knew. Nobody had to try out for the part of Cinderella. I knew whose size-six foot would fit that print—the only guy who wasn't yuk-king it up with the rest of them. Nick really had it in for me.

Mr. Sciarra wasn't looking at the kids. He was trying to think of something nice to say about the flattened clay. "My, that's yet an-other interesting concept, Hobie," he said, and waited for me to explain.

"It's . . ." I stared at Nick, but he wouldn't look me in the eye. Molly did, though, grin-ning. And then Lisa. So did R.X. and Eugene. I guess they were waiting for me to tell on Nick. Mr. Sciarra would get really mad and he's no fun when he's mad.

"It's . . . garbage," I said, because that's what it was.

"Hmmmmmmm. I see. Footstep in mire. Well, I think . . . I think . . . you've captured . . . the essence," Mr. Sciarra said. "Want to fire it?"

"No, thanks," I told him. "Another time." There were a few giggles.

"Since you've finished, Hobie, I wonder if you'd run an errand? Miss Ivanovitch asked me to have two responsible students bring something down from the office to your class." He looked around the floor. "Nick, are you finished with that interesting bowl?"

"Fidished adz I'll ever be," Nick said. His bowl had tiny eyes on its wide rim, huge ears to use as handles, and a long, gross tongue curling out the front. I didn't see a nose.

"Fine. Then you and Hobie go to the office and ask Miss Hutter for the skeleton."

"Excuse me?" I said.

"The skeleton. Miss Ivanovitch wants the skeleton in your room next period, and you're just the guys to carry it with extreme care down the escalator steps."

I didn't look at Nick. I don't know if he looked at me.

40

Eugene was grinning like the Joker. He could hardly wait for Nick and me to punch each other out. I wasn't all that sure anymore that we wouldn't. I mean, my first really good art project all year, and he'd smashed it.

But after all, I decided, Nick is my friend. He probably was just shooting clay balls at me the way we shot spitballs at each other that day Trevor gave his toenail talk. And he probably didn't mean to step on my pizza, just like I didn't mean to snag his nose with a snake. Things happen.

Still, when I swung out the beauty shop door, Nick was at least ten feet behind me. We had to cut through the women's dress department, also known as gym class, to get to the office, which is in Credits and Adjustments.

The fourth graders were playing dodge ball as we ran across the big space. Nick dashed ahead of me, his shoelaces flapping. "Interference!" a kid called. A whistle blew as the ball passed between us.

As soon as we swung the office door open we saw it—a full-sized greeny-cream plastic skeleton standing at the counter, grinning at us with all its teeth showing and all its ribs and toe bones, too. I wondered if it glowed in the dark. Clearly nobody had told it that Central School has this really strict dress code. You've got to wear clothes.

Miss Hutter must have heard me gag when I saw it. She came right out of her office. "Boys," she said, "I expect you've come for Mort. I've been hiding him in my closet."

"Mord?" Nick asked.

"Mort," she said again, grabbing the skeleton by the spine and wheeling it toward us. "I don't remember where he got his name. He's been a part of the fifth-grade curriculum for many years. Do you know yet what his patella is?" she asked.

"His funny bone?" I tried.

She frowned slightly and raised her eyebrows at Nick.

"Id's hids dee cab," Nick told her, and she smiled, either because he got it right or because he sounded so weird.

"How did you hurt yourself, Nick?" Miss Hutter asked.

"Id's nudding," he mumbled.

"He cut it shaving," I told her, but I was the only one who laughed.

Mort was just a little taller than we were, but he cheated: he was on rollers.

"I trust him to your good care," Miss Hutter said as Nick pushed him out of the office. This time, when we crossed through the dodge ball game, the whistle blew, but nobody yelled. The fourth graders just stood there with their jaws hanging, like they'd never seen two kids with a skeleton on wheels before.

When we got to the top of the escalator, we stopped. Since the escalator steps don't move, you've got to walk down them. The skeleton couldn't walk.

"I'll take it from here," I told Nick. "It's easier for just one." When was he going to make his move, I wondered. Would he try to get me at lunch? After school? On the bus?

Some kids in a sixth-grade class on the floor below looked up and saw us there holding this guy with no skin on. I lifted one of his arms and waved at them.

"Hi, Mort," one guy called, remembering him from his fifth-grade parts-of-the-body stuff. "Looking great."

"You carry the tob pard and I'll hold the feed and the stand," Nick said, like he thought I couldn't do it by myself.

I grabbed the ribs, trying to keep Mort's arms from flapping free. Nick raised the legs and the stand. "Ready," he called, and I started moving. The skull stuck out in front of me as I slowly stepped down one stair, two, three, four.

It wasn't just the sixth grade class now; suddenly it was like everybody in the whole school was watching, and they were making *Woooooooooo* ghost sounds every step we took, even though teachers were saying *Shhhhhhh.*

Wooooooshh. It echoed off the department store ceiling and into the three smallest bones in my human body.

The kids who weren't *wooooooing* were laughing. I began to feel dumb. My face was getting hot. I started to move faster.

And then Nick yelled, "Slow dowd!" But I couldn't slow down because he was pushing me. At least he was pushing on his part of the skeleton, and since my part of the skeleton was connected to his part of the skeleton, the bones he was pushing were shoving me down the escalator steps. I grabbed for the railing with one hand, but I was moving too fast to catch it. The other hand was clutching Mort. I couldn't let go of Mort. All I could think of was that Mr. Sciarra and Miss Hutter had warned us to take care of him.

44

The stand flew over my head. Mort's feet flew over my head. *My* feet flew over my head.

When I stopped flying I was heaped at the bottom of the steps. The skeleton's arm was curled round my neck, cold and plastic. Above my eyes a whole mess of silver stars blinked off and on and on and off. Through them I could just make out Nick, shimmering somewhere behind them. It looked like he was grinning.

4. A Bone to Pick

My skull is not cracked. My legs are not broken. My patella is fine, but I'm mad," I told Ms. Kamins. She's the school nurse.

I was lying flat on this cot in what used to be a dressing room at Bob's Togs. The cot was stiff. It didn't like me and I didn't like it.

"That's all right," Ms. Kamins said, patting my shoulder. "Feeling angry is perfectly normal." Ms. Kamins, who's been school nurse since my mom went to Central, always gives advice with her bandages. "We're often angry with ourselves for getting hurt."

"I'm not mad at *myself*," I told her. She smiled.

"Just relax, my dear," she said. "The skeleton took most of the blow. You did, though, have quite a tumble." She smiled again.

"It wasn't funny," I told her. "I don't know why everybody keeps laughing. Falling down an escalator with a skeleton isn't my idea of a big joke."

Making the whole school laugh was bad enough, but that was only part of it. Mostly I was mad because of what Nick had done. It's one thing to fight after school. It's another thing to push a guy down steps. The pushing thing was sneaky. And I felt Nick push, or at least I felt the skeleton push, and I don't think *Mort* thought it up. His brain is clearly missing.

"Did I smash Mort?" I asked. There was such a pile of bones at the foot of the escalator, I couldn't tell how broken up he was.

"Only his left arm," she said, "and I understand Miss Ivanovitch is setting that."

"It's plastic," I told her. "Somehow I don't think plastic works that way."

"And the stand," she went on. "I believe the stand is bent. And of course the hook did crack off the cranium, so the top of his skull is loose. But other than that, and the four missing front teeth, Mort is going to be all right. I expect you are, too. It appears you don't have a concussion, just a scratch or two and a slightly purplish black eye." She looked me over. "You certainly did cause a ruckus, though."

"Will they kill me for smashing him?" I asked her.

"Seems unlikely." She laughed. "Just imprison you here for an hour or so. It was clearly an accident. You had lots of witnesses. They know you didn't push the skeleton off the high dive. Now you just keep your head down and rest awhile." There was a knocking outside the room and she hurried away.

I sat halfway up and saw double. There were two of me, my front and my back reflected in the dressing room mirrors. And then there was the real me in between with a black eye and a spinning head. I put all three heads down on the cot.

Ms. Kamins leaned through the curtained door. "You have a visitor," she said quietly. "Someone is concerned about you and wants to say hello. You feel up to it?"

A visitor. It was Nick, for sure, saying how dumb he was and how he shouldn't have laughed. Or Molly, maybe, apologizing for writing that note. Or Miss Ivanovitch, telling me I didn't have to take the bone test, ever.

"Ohhhhhhh," I moaned, to let whoever it was think I was in really big, big pain. "Ohhhhhhhhhhhh!"

Ms. Kamins grinned at me and ducked back out. Santa Claus came in.

No kidding. Santa Claus. He was the very same one who'd stood on the killer escalator and called "Ho-ho-ho," and told us we were going to get a roomful of computers if we were good boys and girls. When he leaned over me I could tell that his fuzzy, white beard wasn't stuck to his chin, but hooked, somehow, over his head.

"Well, well, Hobie," he said, with a chuckle. His breath smelled like peppermint. "And how are you feeling after that Olympic somersault?"

How did this fat guy in a red suit know my name? Did he really know all? Was he making a list and checking it twice, writing it down who was naughty or nice? If he was, the list said that in the last two days I'd dug up a time capsule after I'd promised not to, that I'd landed Nick in the nose with a poisonous snake, and that I'd maimed the school skeleton. Or maybe I was just dreaming. I closed my eyes and bit my tongue. It hurt. When I opened my eyes, my tongue still hurt and Santa Claus was sitting down in the folding chair next to the cot.

"I am feeling," I told him, "funny."

"You *look* funny, too. You've got a black eye," he said in this squeaky voice I'd heard somewhere before. Then he began to kind of sing, "Mort fell down and broke his crown and you came tumbling after." But his lips weren't moving. When I turned my head I could see that it was Oscar, the fuzzy-headed puppet, talking. This weird wooden head had its mouth open wide enough to swallow an apple whole.

"It's not polite to laugh at people who have black eyes," I told the puppet as though he was real.

"Your eye is black and you are blue," the puppet said, clicking his teeth. Santa Claus kept a stiff smile when the puppet talked, but his lips were pretty still. He was good at this.

"Now, Oscar, let the boy be," he said,

sounding like a nice old man. "We came by from our North Pole annex," he told me, "because we saw you fall."

I leaned forward on my elbow. "Santa Claus," I told him, "I hate to tell you this, but I don't believe in you. I haven't believed in you since I was four years old and found my presents in a closet the week before Christmas. One of them was an excellent yellow dump truck, which I gave to Toby Rossi last summer."

"*I* remember that truck," the puppet chirped. "It was swell. Unc, this lad doesn't think you're real. He doesn't know you watched him fall with your X-ray vision."

Something was wrong here. How could Santa Claus have seen me take those steps? He wasn't in school. If he *had* been, the kids would have been watching him, not me.

"Wait a minute," I said to the puppet. "That's Superman who has X-ray vision."

"All right." Oscar faced me. "Explain how Santa Claus sees you when you're sleeping and knows when you're awake?"

I sat up. The dizziness had gone away, though in the mirror I could still see my purple eye. "You may not be Santa Claus," I told him, "but I know you. I've seen you someplace before."

"In a store window?" Oscar asked. I rolled my eyes. "Sliding down your chimney on a cold winter's night?" he tried.

"We don't have a fireplace. You should know that."

"Just about time for me to be getting back," Santa Claus said and stood up, like he was about to leave.

I stood up, too. "No kidding, how did you know I'd fallen?"

"Well," he said, with a kind of sigh, "Santa Claus usually keeps those secrets, but since I'm here to cheer you up, I'll tell. I saw you when I was taking an igloo break. Gets very hot in there."

"And he was as tired as Mort," Oscar interrupted.

"How tired is that?" Santa asked him.

"Bone tired!" He stretched his mouth into a wide guffaw. "Haw haw!"

"Oscar, Oscar," Santa said. "Well, I took my break in a special secluded place. I was sitting in the dark in one of those small rooms where store detectives used to sit looking out onto the first floor. They watched for shoplifters there when this was Bob's Togs."

"You mean the spy place," I told him. "Nick discovered that the first day we were here, and he and I climbed up and looked down from it. From the floor you think it's just an air vent, but it's really this terrific place to spy from. You can see practically everybody." I shrugged. "They don't let us go there anymore."

"I wasn't spying," Santa Claus said, "just resting my feet and looking over the younger generation."

"Stores don't use those peepholes to look for shoplifters anymore," I told him. "They're old-fashioned. My dad said. In modern-type stores they use cameras. You look up when you're in almost any other store in the mall. You'll see." He frowned, like something I'd said was wrong. It wasn't, though. I'd seen those cameras scoping out places. "How'd *you* know it was there, the spy place?" I asked him. "I bet not many people do."

"Ah," he said, and taking his red cap off, he pulled it over Oscar's head and put his puppet hand behind his back. Then, whispering like he didn't want Oscar to hear, he said, "You're right. I'm not the real Santa Claus."

Making his voice even softer, he went on, "I'm 'Bob' Bobb, and since this is *my* 'old-fashioned' store, I know every nook and cranny."

"Let me *outta* here!" Oscar yelled, his voice muffled, and Santa brought his arm back round.

Once I knew, I could tell it was him. He was in our class on our first day at Bob's Togs. I hoped he wasn't mad at me. Anyway, it was true, the store *was* old-fashioned. At supper one night practically all my mom and dad talked about was how Bob's had gone broke because it was so old-fashioned.

Since this guy was Mr. Bobb, that meant the Santa belly wasn't padded. I'd seen him in his real clothes, which were size huge.

"I should have known all along," I told him. "But I never saw you like this. Do you do the igloo thing every year?"

He looked in the mirror, adjusted his beard a little, and said, "No. I've thought about it before, but this is my first time as Jolly Old Saint Nicholas. Being retired and all, I thought it would be a fine way to celebrate the season." He sank into the folding chair.

"Well, is it fun? Did you have to go to Santa Claus school?"

"I wish I had," he said. "Maybe it would have helped. They just told me to give each child three requests and then say I'd do my best to deliver. They fixed me up with a suit and beard and I dug Oscar out of an old trunk. I expect he'd been packed inside for forty years." He held the puppet up and polished its cheeks with the fur on his sleeve. "As for being fun, well, I don't know. I can't seem to get the knack of it."

"I thought you did fine on the escalator," I said. "That was a good one you told us about the choking and joking." I meant it. It *was* pretty good. A lot of people laughed.

He looked proud. "Oscar remembers a lot of his old jokes. That's not really the problem. The problem is with the boys and girls. They aren't like the children I used to know. You seem like a sensible boy. Can you explain what's happened to the youth of today?"

"Listen, kids are just kids," I told him. "You'll get used to them."

He smiled weakly and shook his head, like he didn't believe it for a minute. How do you cheer up a sad Santa Claus, anyway? I changed the subject. "You been doing funny voices a long time?" I asked.

It did brighten him up. "I taught myself

when I was your age. I read a book on ventriloquism and practiced until my dogs Pete and Moss could tell each other jokes." He turned to Oscar. "Why do tiny dogs make good radio announcers?" he asked.

Oscar opened his mouth wide, clapped it shut, and then said, "Because they have wee paws for station identification." I knew that joke. I told it myself when I was a kid, only I said TV instead of radio. We all laughed.

Ms. Kamins hurried back in the room. "Bob," she said to Santa Claus, "while it's extremely thoughtful of you to visit Hobie, he really should be resting. And so, I think, should you. You look bushed. It's just possible you haven't the stamina for this."

Ms. Kamins put her hands on her hips like she was deciding what to do about us. "I tell you what," she said. "How about if I pop over to the cafeteria and get you both some nice cold chocolate milk?"

While Santa Claus was nodding yes, Oscar leaned toward me and whispered, "I wooden like it."

"Yes, thanks," I said, laughing, and Oscar pulled his mouth wide in amazement. Ms. Kamins hurried off.

"You sorry you closed the store?" I asked Santa Bobb, once she'd gone.

He crossed his arms, tucking Oscar behind him. "Well," he sighed, "what's done's done. That's what I always say. Bob's Togs was in the family for forty years. I ran it for twenty, just the way my daddy did before me. Then, three years ago, my nephew Rob joined the business with me and we moved away from Main Street into this fancy mall. I made the new Bob's as much like the old one as I could."

He got up and looked around. "I could have saved money in a lot of ways. I could have made this very dressing room smaller. But I built a good solid store. Rob said my methods weren't up to date. He said my togs were old-fashioned."

To be nice I should have told him he was right and his nephew was wrong, but Mom and Dad had said exactly what his nephew had, so I kept my mouth shut.

He still hadn't told me if he was sorry he'd closed the store, but it sounded like he was.

"That nephew of mine," he went on, "said I was just an old fogey living in the middle ages." He was shaking his Oscar hand at me, but the puppet wasn't talking. "And Rob did something that was . . . that was unforgivable."

I thought about it. "He didn't push you down the escalator steps, did he?" I wasn't so sure I could forgive that.

"Of course not," he said. "He up and left. And then he opened Rob's Togs for Polliwogs in another mall—clothes for children. People stopped coming here. I think they started going there instead. But the Polliwog place is absurd. His window mannequins either hang upside down or they're robots that walk on their hands, stick out their tongues, and wiggle their ears. Their noses spin round and round. That's no way to sell clothing."

Sounded great to me. "Do people buy his stuff?"

"I don't know. We're not speaking."

"Did you hit him?" I asked.

He looked at me like I was bonkers. "I abhor violence. That's why I'm so impressed with your school—because the children wrote me such cordial letters and because I've not seen any of them fighting."

He really *was* Santa Claus, after all. "I bet

it's *you* giving us the computers, and not the mall."

"It's me," he said, scratching under his wig with the Oscar hand. I looked up and laughed, it was so weird.

He saw me look, realized what he was doing, and smiled. "Get me down," Oscar yelled, peering over his forehead. "I'm scared of heights. This is too hairy!"

Santa swooped him down like he was landing a jet, and we both laughed.

Ms. Kamins came back in and gave us each a carton with a striped straw. "Santa, my friend," she said, "they're asking for you in the mall. A long line is forming in front of your igloo, and the children are turning surly. Two mothers are chanting 'San-ta, San-ta.' After this bit of refreshment," she went on, "I expect it's time for you both to get back to work."

I guess it was. It sure was time for me to show Nick, once and for all, that he couldn't kick me down the stairs. I had a bone to pick and I was going to do a whole lot more about it than stop talking to him.

"Will you be all right?" I asked Santa Bobb.

"I don't know," he said. "The children speak

a language of toys I don't understand. They don't say please. They don't say thank you."

He tucked Oscar in his pocket, stood up, shook his head, and said, "I'll try once more. Feel well, young man. I enjoyed our chat. Can I count on you to keep up that fine behavior?"

I didn't say no. That would be like saying I didn't want the computers. But I had to punch Nick out. So, I didn't say yes, either. He seemed like such a nice old guy that I smiled and kind of waved, figuring that could mean anything.

"Can I count on *you* to get me outta here?" Oscar yelled from his pocket. "I'm giving you ten. One, two, three . . ." And they both left for the igloo, counting on each other.

5. In a Pickle

Even with four front teeth gone, Mort was grinning. He was sitting in Miss Ivanovitch's chair, his feet propped up on her desk. A Cubs' cap with the bill to the back was tilted on his skull. His left arm was slung in a flowered scarf with a long fringe.

"Hobie," Miss Ivanovitch called out when she saw me, "we're glad *your* skeleton isn't broken. Mort came down with a cracked funny bone. But Ms. Kamins told us you'd survived with only a—"

"Racoon eye," R.X. said.

"Prune eye." That was Molly. A lot of kids giggled behind their hands.

Nick was right in front of me. "How you do-id?" he asked.

As if he cared how I was doing. I didn't answer him. I did detour down the next aisle so he wouldn't be able to stick out his foot to try and trip me.

"All right, class, let's get back to the test," Miss Ivanovitch said. "I have only a couple of questions left. Hobie, I expect you've had about as much bone stress today as you need. You can take a different test tomorrow morning before class when I talk with Amber."

It would be good to come in with Amber. She's this kid who's got some kind of learning problem that keeps her from reading and writing very well. Miss Ivanovitch always goes over written tests with her. If I took the test while they were talking, maybe I could figure out some of the answers. Also, if I came in early, I wouldn't have to hang around outside after getting off the bus, freezing and waiting to get into a fight.

As I passed Lisa on my way back to my seat, she said, "I know something you don't know."

"Wanta bet?" She probably thought I couldn't figure out exactly what was going on with Nick.

I slumped down in my seat. The note from Molly was still on my desk. I stuck it in my pocket. As I watched everybody write stuff down about fibulas and tibulas, I wondered why they didn't call the chest bones ribulas.

"All right," Miss Ivanovitch said, "here's the last question. While it may help if you saw the Bears play the Vikings last night, you should, with a hint, be able to answer it. What bone did fullback Truck Mansfield break?"

Almost everybody groaned as if they were the ones whose bone was broken.

"Enough, enough. Here's the hint. It was the biggest bone in his right leg."

"What's it start with?" Eugene asked.

"It starts with his knee."

"No, I mean . . ."

"I know what you mean. Just answer the question."

"How long's he going to be out?" somebody asked.

"The rest of the season," she said. "Bones like that take a long time to knit. That's unlike Mort's break, which ought to be cured by tomorrow."

"How'd you fix him?" I asked her.

"Krazy Glue," she said. "I'm going to play

dentist, too, as soon as we find his teeth. Remember, everybody, please look for teeth on your way down from lunch. They're probably caught in the ridges of the escalator steps."

"Disgusting," somebody said.

"And now the last half of the last question," she went on. "Truck Mansfield's bone snapped in two, but did not break the skin. What kind of fracture is that?"

"That's an ow-wee, a very bad ow-wee," Marshall answered out loud.

"Be sure you spell it right," she told him, grinning. "When you're finished, pass your papers to the front."

As the tests were moving up, I saw Lisa lean forward and whisper something in Molly's ear. Then Lisa whipped out another sheet of paper and started to write. Molly glared at her as if Lisa had said she was going to print "Kick Me" on Molly's back with a permanent Magic Marker. "Don't you *dare*," Molly whispered low. Lisa kept writing.

Miss Ivanovitch stacked the tests on her desk and placed Mort's free hand on them as a paperweight.

Molly narrowed her eyes at Lisa, reached back, grabbed the paper, and crumpled it in her fist. "I said *no,*" she hissed. Then she put her hand in the dark cave of her desk and drew out what looked like a green pickle.

Lisa was fuming, but she could hardly raise her hand and say Molly had torn up a note she was going to pass.

A lot of us were watching them, including Miss Ivanovitch. "Molly," she said, "we're about to explore the remarkable world of the May-flower. From your reading, could you tell us what you might *not* have liked about living on board the ship?"

Molly had to regroup. You can't stay mad and tell what you would have hated about sailing in a leaky boat three hundred seventy-some years ago. And Molly wanted to tell.

"Well," she sighed, "it was gross. For starters, you had worms in your bread and maggots in your meat. And the first sailor up in the morning was called the Cruncher because when he walked across the deck he crunched cockroaches."

"Eeuuuuuuu." Lisa put her fingers in her ears.

But Molly was just getting warmed up. "You had to go to the toilet in a bucket; there wasn't any water to wash in, so you didn't wash; and if you got sick, which you probably did, you threw up on your shoes. That's why this sailor on the Mayflower called the Pilgrims 'puke stockings.' "

"Did she make that up?" R.X. asked.

Molly looked straight at him. "The sailor who called them that died and they thought it served him right."

A kid in back raised his hand. "I always thought the Pilgrims were good friends, but I guess not."

"They certainly did argue, it's true," Miss Ivanovitch said. "But they also decided that if they didn't agree on some things, they'd probably all die." She walked down our aisle. "That's why they made up some rules before they landed. Anybody know what the agreement was called?" She headed to the other side of the room. "Jessica?"

While Jessica, this shy kid, was practically whispering about what the Pilgrims said they'd do together when they got off the boat, Molly picked up the green pickle again, turned around, aimed it at Lisa, and squeezed. The pickle squeaked and squirted at the same time.

Lisa raised both hands and shrieked. "Miss Ivanovitch, Molly sprayed stuff at me. And it's gross stuff. She's completely disgusting. She ought to get expelled from school forever and ever. At least from our class. At least from this row." She stood up so all of the class could see that she had a small damp stain on her pink T-shirt, belly high.

"It's her fault," Molly said. "She was writing a note about me."

"It was a true note," Lisa said, "and she stole it and tore it up."

"My dears," Miss Ivanovitch told them, "as you well know, neither note passing nor pickle squirting is in order. We are talking about sailing the high seas in the dead of winter on the way to a new land." She walked over to them. "I take it the note is gone, but I'll confiscate the pickle."

Molly held it close. "It was a gift. My grandmother gave it to me for my birthday last weekend. She gave me that, a red dirt bike and a set of encyclopedias through the letter P."

Miss Ivanovitch held out her hand. "Then with a brand new bike and half a mine of knowledge you won't miss one pickle too much," she said.

"My grandmother," Molly went on, "thought

this pickle was very very funny. She said when she was young, all they had were water pistols."

"Is that what's in it?" Miss Ivanovitch asked. "Water?"

Molly shrugged. "Actually, no, it's got pickle juice," she told her. "But it's good clean dill pickle juice . . . with garlic." She held the squirter close.

"Molly!" Miss Ivanovitch warned, and Molly sighed and gave it to her.

"Can I have it back after school?" she asked.

"In fact, you may not. The pickle," Miss Ivanovitch said, "is going straight into the June Box," and she walked over to this cardboard carton. It's high on a bookcase near the chalkboard that separates our class from Mr. Star's fourth grade.

"Oh, no," Molly moaned, "not the June Box."

"Ah," Lisa said with a smile, "the June Box."

Everything that's dropped in the June Box stays there until the last day of school. It's stuff that Miss Ivanovitch has taken away in class— not food or things that would mold and turn gross, but stuff like bouncing bloodshot eyeballs, and metal crickets and bubble makers, and boxes that you flip to make cow noises, and those whirling circles that spark when you pump them with your thumb.

Miss Ivanovitch stepped out of her shoes, climbed on a chair, and dropped the plastic pickle in.

"It's *seven months* to June," Molly wailed.

Lisa smiled and rubbed the pickle juice stain, which was fading fast.

"My grandmother is going to be mad. When she gave that to me she laughed so hard I thought she was going to fall off the sofa," Molly said. "If *she* thought it was funny, I don't see why you don't think it's funny."

Miss Ivanovitch climbed down from the chair and put her shoes back on. "It may well be funny. Another day, in another place, perhaps even in another galaxy, a squirt pickle filled with eau de garlic would be a joy to us all, but not here. Not now."

Molly narrowed her eyes at Lisa, like it was *her* fault she'd lost her pickle. Lisa kicked the back of her chair.

As Miss Ivanovitch was beginning again, asking about the Mayflower Compact, Eugene turned to me and whispered, "When you guys going to fight? Nick said he didn't think you'd do it."

I shrugged. "What does he think I am, scared?" If I wanted to I could just ask Nick over after school to find out what was going on, but I sure didn't want him thinking I was chicken.

"Okay, what is it, noon on the parking lot, or not?" Now Eugene sounded mad.

The mall's back parking lot is where they send us after lunch. They've blocked off space for us to hang out there instead of cruising the mall. If we were going to fight, that was as good a place as any.

"Okay," I told him, "high noon on the parking lot. Pass it on." My banged-up eye felt hot. I stared across the room at Nick. He was staring back. His nose was glowing.

6. Nick at Noon

If the snow had been as high as our armpits, Miss Hutter might have switched on the bullhorn and said, "Attention, people, only polar bears are allowed outside. You'll have to spend your lunchtime in the toasty mall shops. Be sure to get a fat, warm cinnamon bun, my treat." She might have said that, if the snow had been up to our armpits, but it wasn't.

You could bring your own bag of food or buy lunch upstairs in the Bob's kids' clothes department cafeteria. I bought two hot dogs, a paper cup of french fries, a peanut butter cookie, size extra large, and a big yellow apple with one bruise to match my eye. I wasn't sure if it meant I was chicken or not, but I just didn't feel like fighting. I sat down and began to eat as slowly as I could. No big deal, except that everybody else finished eating in two seconds, practically inhaling whole bologna sandwiches and sword-swallowing their carrot sticks. Eugene didn't even bother to pull his Oreos apart and lick the icing first. Between gulps they were talking about our weird Santa Claus on the escalator and his even weirder puppet. I didn't say much. I sure didn't tell them who Santa Claus really was. That was my secret. Nobody mentioned Nick and me fighting. I figured they'd forgotten.

But suddenly all the talk stopped and there was this long silence aimed straight at me. I'd figured wrong. I threw a soggy french fry into the air and caught it on my tongue.

"So, what's taking you so long, Hanson?" Eugene asked, making a big deal out of it. Everybody else at the table had already finished eating and tossed their garbage in the trash. They stared at me. I folded the french fry between my teeth and chewed it twenty times.

"Yeah, Nick's gone outside," Trevor said,

punching my sore ribs with his elbow. I looked across the room. Nick was gone, all right. He must not have eaten at all.

"Probably he's standing around in the cold getting madder and madder." Rolf stood up, pushed his chair in, and waited.

They expected me to do something. So I stuffed the whole peanut butter cookie into my mouth until my cheeks puffed out like a trumpet player's. Then I shoved the apple into my pocket and pushed back from the table. I mean, no matter how slowly I chewed, there was still no way I could eat up the entire lunch hour. Sooner or later they make you go outside.

While I was washing the last of the cookie down with milk, Molly came over and sat in the chair across from me.

"Hobie," she said, "I've made up my mind that you won't be fighting Nick at noon, even though everybody says you're going to," like it was hers to decide.

The guys groaned.

"I thought you were mad at me," I said.

"I am. I think you're a dwerp, but that doesn't have anything to do with it. It would be amazingly stupid to fight Nick."

"How come?" Eugene said, standing up to go.

"Why?" I asked, hoping she had about three really good reasons.

"I've got three really good reasons," she told me, and the guys at the table groaned again, louder.

"Like what?" I wanted to know. I really wanted to know.

"Like, one, you just fell down and broke your crown and who knows what else. The nurse should have sent you home."

"You mean you're worried about me getting hurt?" I asked. That was nice. That was *very* nice. She didn't hate me at all. She was just saying she did.

"Number two, you've doubled Nick's nose size already and fighting him might make it even bigger."

"You're worried about me beating Nick up?" She thought I was stronger than Nick and he didn't have a chance. This was better than I thought.

"Come on, cut it out," Eugene told her. "Nick is already outside waiting for Hobie. No way he can back out now."

"Reason two-and-a-half," Molly went on,

"Miss Ivanovitch would keep you after school forever."

"Enough," Rolf said. "Miss Ivanovitch doesn't count. Hobie can't get out of it."

"How come she doesn't count?" I asked, but he didn't answer.

"Three." Molly isn't easy to stop. "Three, if there's fighting in the parking lot, we might not get those computers from the mall. Did you ever think about that? Did you? That Santa Claus person sounded like the computers were rewards for *not* fighting." She crossed her arms like this was the clincher. "I don't want Nick and Hobie to mess it up for the rest of us."

She wasn't worried about me at all. She just wanted to be sure she was going to have a screen light up and talk to her and tell her all her answers were perfect.

"So this last reason, it's the real one, right?" I asked her.

"Well . . ." she said, shrugging, "it's—"

"He called me names," I told her. "He called me a—"

"So what?" she said. "Sticks and stones can break my bones, but words can never hurt me. That's what my grandmother says."

"A lot she knows," I told Molly. "I hate it when people call me names. It stinks."

"It wasn't words that got you that black eye, though," she said. And she laughed.

"Nick did that, too. He pushed me down the steps," I told her. "You think I should just take that?"

"*Pushed* you?"

"No kidding?" Eugene sounded like he thought that was absolutely terrific. "So he hit you first? He's got it coming."

"That's that, then," Trevor shoved in his chair and headed away from the table. "You got to fight back for something like that."

"Are you sure he pushed you?" Molly grabbed my arm.

"Sure I'm sure. I fell, didn't I?"

"That means it was *his* fault the skeleton broke, too," Trevor said. "And, think about it, it could have been *your* front teeth we're collecting from the escalator treads. I never liked Nick."

"Me neither," Eugene said.

"Well, I do," Molly said.

"I don't," I told her. "Not anymore." The guys were right. I had to do it. Nick was mad at me for something I didn't do on purpose. That was dumb. He told Molly something I asked him especially not to tell her. That was mean. He threw clay balls at my ear and stepped in my pizza. That was disgusting. But worst of all, he pushed me down the steps. That was crazy. Nobody liked him but Molly, and possibly his mother. And maybe R.X., who ate lunch with him. But they were wrong. It was time for me to smear Nick.

I got up, grabbed my coat off the chair, and headed down the escalator steps, holding on to both banisters as I went.

Nobody pushed me, but I did have this line of kids behind me like I was the Pied Piper blowing rats out of Hamelin. As we filed down one escalator, a sixth-grade class was climbing up the other.

"Hey, it's fifth-grade follow the leader," a tall kid called. "Whatever you do, don't do what that klutz does." He pointed at me. "He'll crack you up."

A girl leaned toward me. "We're going to give Mort a new name now that you've broken him," she said. "We've decided on Bonaparte. Get it, bone-apart?" All the kids around her got it and laughed.

"Wook at that, wittle baby Hobie gots to hold

on to both rails," one guy said, talking cute, and I let go.

"You know what I hear? I hear Hobie's going to run away from home and join the circus as an acrobat."

"Must have flipped his lid like Mort did." They laughed. The whole sixth grade sounded like they were starting a Guinness Book of World Records of Ways to Zap Hobie. If I didn't give them something else to think about me, it would never end. I would hear it on the bus. I would hear it on the playground. They would tell it everywhere. When I graduated from high school somebody would say, "Remember the day Hanson took a dive with the skeleton on the escalator?"

I waved. I smiled. I crossed my eyes at the sixth graders all the way down, like I thought it was just great being the guy that made everybody laugh their heads off. Then across the ground floor we marched, out to war, me on the good side, Nick on the bad. Except for Molly, my troops were cheering me on.

Eugene ran ahead and swung open the loading dock door that led to the parking lot playground. The other kids hung back. I walked out into the cold alone.

It was still snowing hard. The plows must have been at work all morning long, though, clearing bus paths and shoving drifts aside so we would have room to fool around on the blacktop. In the middle of the parking lot a huge mound of icy snow—at least eight feet high—had been pushed up against a light pole. A bunch of kids hung around the base of it looking up. At the top of the pile, leaning out from the pole, holding on with one gloved hand, was Nick. He was king of the mountain.

He was king for now, but he sure wasn't going to be for long.

7. Greatest Hero of the Maul

I headed straight for the foot of the icy mountain, my parade behind me. Nick swung around the pole, laughing with R.X. and the group of kids at the bottom of the snow heap. None of them was trying to knock him down. They were all on his side.

At the next mound over, I could see two adult types huddled together talking. I bet those teachers didn't even guess there was going to be a huge fight practically under their cold noses.

"Nick thinks he's so great standing way up there," Eugene whispered. "That's a humongous mountain. I bet he doesn't believe you can hit him that high."

"Go get him," Trevor said. "All he's king of is the chicken heap. Cluuuck-cluckcluck-cluck."

Nick's kids moved toward us. "We thought you weren't coming," R.X. called. "He's been waiting for you about twenty minutes. It's way after noon."

Nick couldn't possibly have been there twenty minutes. Five maybe. Ten at the outside.

Molly dashed in front of me, grabbed my cap, and tucked it under her jacket. "Your ears are going to freeze. If I were you, I'd get my cap and forget about fighting," she said, and then she raced away.

"You aren't me," I called. "You aren't even close." Snow was dropping on my head in fat clumps. Either I went off on a wild cap chase the way Molly meant me to, or pretty soon my hair would turn totally white. I wasn't about to run. So what if I had giant dandruff?

I folded my arms and looked up.

The snow mound where Nick stood reached way higher than my head, but its sides weren't frozen hard yet. To get to the top, all I had to do was kick footholds into it. I thwacked my toe hard near the base. The snow sank in far enough so I could step up about eight inches.

"That's one small step for boy, one giant leap for boykind," I said, thinking maybe Nick would laugh.

He leaned against the pole and stared at me. "R.X. said you said I was a liar," he called down. He was not laughing.

When did I say he was a liar? I didn't remember telling R.X. Nick was a liar. He *was* a liar, but I didn't remember saying it. I kicked in another shoe cave and pulled higher, hugging the mound with my arms. A chunk of snow caught inside my right sneaker and slush began to ooze down my heel.

"Trevor said you said you were going to get me," I yelled straight into the hill, but Nick could hear. I knew he could. "He said you said I stink."

"Trevor told me what you told him," Nick went on.

I couldn't remember what I'd told Trevor. "And I'll do it, too," I said, figuring that covered just about anything. I smashed in another step and dragged myself up. My head was level with his feet, not a highly smart place for a head to be.

"You know that worm you gave my brother? It died in his pocket and he cried, and that stinks," Nick called down. "And *it* stinks because he won't throw it away."

I felt bad about that. I like Toby. If he wasn't so gross, he'd be an okay kid. I couldn't tell Nick I felt bad about it, though. That didn't have anything to do with this.

"You pushed me down the escalator," I shouted at his black high-toppers. "And I bet you knew when you did it that I could have died as dead as that worm."

"I did what?"

"You know what." The snow under my feet began to crumble. I grabbed his ankle to keep from falling, and he must not have been holding on really tight to the pole because just as soon as I grabbed, I slipped and he slipped with me. I searched for a toehold, but it was too late. What goes up must come down, and we were coming down. Fast. I tobogganed to the bottom on my belly. Nick slid down behind me on his back. Kids scrambled to the sides to make a path as we careened past.

When I stopped, my head was resting on somebody's wet gym shoe. A couple of kids were cheering. I opened my eyes to see why and watched as Molly, finding the throne empty, scrambled up my carefully kicked-in steps like she had spikes on her toes. She was wearing my cap. With Nick and me spread out at the bottom, Molly made it to the top. Hugging the pole with both arms, she crouched low, set to kick out at the first kid who tried to take her place. "There now," she said, "that's better."

"You can't be king of the mountain," R.X. called. "You're a girl."

She thought a second. "Who wants to be king, anyway? I'm the monarch. It sounds better. Monarch of the mountain." She whirled around to check her position from all sides. Nobody was starting up to heave her off.

That's because almost everybody was watching Nick and me. We both got up slow, hemmed in by a crowd of kids who'd heard we were going to fight. They'd got themselves ringside seats, standing room only.

Nick held up his fists and started to dance around like the guys do on TV.

"Cream him, Hobie," I heard behind me.

"Get him, Nick," a girl yelled.

I put my fists up and started to dance, too.

I didn't want to hit him on the nose. It already looked gross enough. So I jerked my arm back and smashed it toward his shoulder, figuring I could whirl him down if not out. He moved and I missed.

Nick didn't miss. He smashed me on the arm and I spun back, feeling the sting.

Kids all around us were yelling. Soon the teachers would be there. A ring of kids screaming had to mean something was happening that shouldn't be. I clenched my teeth, looked Nick straight in the eye, and got ready to deliver the one-two punch. But before I could, I heard this high, sharp shriek and a "Get out of my waaay!"

The Monarch of the Mountain was giving up her throne. Molly raced down the snowy slope, through the crowd of kids, and into the middle of our ring. I could tell she was going to do something stupid like when she stole my cap, and I opened my mouth to tell her to get out of my way and to do it right now.

She slid to an ice skater's stop between Nick and me. Then, without a second breath, without giving either of us time to think about what might happen next, she slammed out her fists and hit us both on our jaws like she was this major world power.

She got *both* of us. We never expected it. She took us by surprise is all. Plus the ground was slick, very extremely slick—ice, actually. It's hard to stand up on ice even if nobody's hit you, but when somebody shoves you as hard as she possibly can and you don't know she's going to, you just naturally fall down.

We fell down. She'd leveled us, zapped us right off our feet. We flew back and slid in opposite directions, down and out. We weren't out cold, but we were cold, for sure. As we bounced across the bumpy snow, the circle of kids opened up. I could hear their shouts and, I think, cheers. I saw lots of cloudy sky up above.

Suddenly the cheering and shouting stopped flat, like it was only sound effects and someone had cut the switch. Then, just as suddenly, somebody said, "And what, I would like to know, is *this* all about?"

A face came between me and the gray sky. It was the face that belonged to the question. It was Ms. O'Malley, one of the teachers. She'd probably been stationed at the next mound of snow. You didn't mess with her. I started to lift myself up to try to explain that we were

just fooling around in the snow, just being fun-loving, regular-guy kids.

Then I saw another face next to hers. It was the guy she'd been talking to on the playground, except he wasn't a teacher at all. He was my old friend Robert "Bob" Bobb, who didn't look like Santa Claus anymore. His cheeks were still North Pole red, but in his black overcoat and fat raccoon cap with ear flaps, he could have been wearing another disguise. Maybe puppets hibernate in the cold, because Oscar was nowhere in sight.

Mr. Bobb glanced at Molly, who was standing with her hands on her hips. Then he looked back and forth at Nick and me lying flat on the snow-covered blacktop.

"I'm waiting for your answers," Ms. O'Malley said. "What is going on here?"

"Nothing," I explained, sitting up carefully.

"Nothing," Nick told her, raising himself and rubbing his chin.

"Nothing?" she asked, looking round the circle of kids.

"Molly punched them out," R.X. said, "that's what." He blinked, like it was him she'd hit. "They were going to punch each other out but she did it for them."

"She got a double knockout," Eugene said, staring at Molly like she'd just swooped down in a UFO and ray-gunned us. "She was incredible. We thought it was going to be Nick and Hobie, but she didn't even give them a chance. She was amazing."

Molly smiled at him.

"Do I understand that you hit these boys, young lady?" Mr. Bobb asked her. "You were fighting?"

Molly raised her chin and nodded. This was glory.

"I'm disappointed," he said. "I'm genuinely disappointed." He didn't look at all jolly.

"You three come with me," Ms. O'Malley told us. "The rest of you tend to your own business. We're going to get to the bottom of this."

This had already gotten to the bottom of me. I was sore. Still, I scrambled to my feet. Kids began to wander off, a lot of them walking backward, though, to watch what would happen to us.

"We were just fooling around," I explained as we headed toward school. Mr. Bobb was walking with us.

"Somehow, it didn't sound like fooling," he said. "It sounded like fighting." He put his hand on my shoulder. "I'm especially sorry that you were involved. I had thought better of you than this."

I was sorry, too. I liked him. I mean, he'd been really nice to me after I'd bounced down the steps. I even knew what he meant about kids being pretty gross sometimes. But they can't be like store mannequins with their mouths always set in a smile. Neither can adults, for that matter.

"They were practically going to kill each other," Molly told Mr. Bobb. "And I stopped them."

"To stop the boys from fighting, you hit them? Did I get that right?" Ms. O'Malley asked.

Molly beamed, clearly pleased with herself.

Mr. Bobb shook his head. "In my day, young lady, little girls did not engage in fisticuffs."

"No," Molly said. "I don't suppose they did."

I didn't believe him. I bet he'd just forgotten.

A bunch of kids ran yelling past us.

"In my day," Mr. Bobb went on, "we used to form two straight lines to file back into school. One was the boys' line, the other was the girls'. We were silent, I remember."

"Those were the old days," Molly said.

"The *good* old days," he told her.

"Maybe not," she said, pulling my cap down over her ears.

I poked her to get her to quit. She didn't know who she was talking back to. She didn't even pretend she hadn't hit us. And she was the one who said she was worried about Nick and me fighting the school out of a ton of computers. She didn't know this guy was "Bob" Bobb, Santa Claus, and the computer Tooth Fairy all wrapped up in a black overcoat. She didn't know she was making one *big* mistake.

8. Take the Freight Elevator Up and Out

Ms. O'Malley aimed us toward the freight elevator and told us to wait inside. "You sit down and stay put and don't even *think* about fighting. You hear?" she said. "Very soon, *very* soon, Miss Ivanovitch will be here to deal with you."

Deal? What kind of deal, I wondered. Big deal, maybe.

"Yes, Ms. O'Malley," Molly answered. She was loving this. She was loving it all.

The elevator was huge. They used to use it when the place was still a store, to haul long racks of winter coats to the second floor or send up big boxes of socks. Actually, it was big enough to hold a couple of pretty good-sized elephants, if they ever wanted to have a two-for-the-price-of-one elephant sale. Fat brown quilts covered the elevator walls and batches of folding chairs were stacked in back. The place was a padded cell and just as soundproof.

I'd already spent some time in the elevator. That's where I took saxophone lessons with five other kids. The story was that the quilts were left hanging in the elevator when we moved in and, instead of pulling them down, some teacher decided it was just the place for kids to take their violin, saxophone, and drum lessons. That way the rest of the school could get through whole days without having to plug their ears with their thumbs. Noise carries like crazy on the big open floor at Bob's, and five minutes of just my blowing saxophone scales could have soured hundreds of kids on music forever.

Nick lifted a white metal chair from the stack and set it up in the corner. "She told us to sit," he said, then sat and looked at his feet.

"If I screamed, would anyone hear me?" Molly asked. She was still wearing my cap.

"If I pushed button two, would the elevator

go up?" I asked Nick. "You think we'd zap through the roof like a rocket? Maybe this is really a time machine, and if we pressed the right button, we'd time bend into the forty-first century." Nick kept staring at the sole of his sneaker like it had a list of bones he was memorizing.

Okay, he wasn't going to talk to me. I could play that game. I turned away from him to Molly. "What do you think they're going to do to us?"

"Nothing," she said. "Not to me, anyway. What could they do? All I did was stop World War Three between you and Nick."

Nick looked up and shook his head.

"Maybe I'll get a medal," she went on, "or a gift certificate from the mall for a macadamia nut cookie and a Diet Coke. That would be nice."

"Wait a minute," I told her. "You were caught fighting. You were caught red-handed. R.X. and Eugene told on you."

"You are totally wrong," she said. "I wasn't fighting. I was *stopping* a fight. I don't even know why I'm here with you criminals, except maybe as a witness. I think I'll go complain to Miss Hutter." She took off my cap and tossed it to me like a Frisbee, but she didn't move fast. Molly always wanted to be where things were happening.

Still, she was edging down the hallway that led to the school, when I saw Miss Ivanovitch hurrying toward us. Amber and Marshall followed close behind her. Amber and Marshall were wearing bright blue sweatshirts that said in big black letters "MEDIATOR." Those must have been the presents Miss Ivanovitch had told them they'd get at noon.

Miss Ivanovitch was biting her lip, always a bad sign.

"Can we really do it now?" Marshall was asking. "We just finished training."

Training? What was he going to do to us?

"Couldn't we start with an easier one?" Amber asked.

"Molly, we need you here," Miss Ivanovitch said, as Molly tried to pass her.

"I'm going to see Miss Hutter," Molly said, "to complain."

"You'll have to stand in line," Miss Ivanovitch told her. "Mr. Bobb is currently talking to her about this little girl who was fighting on the playground."

"What little girl?"

"It seems that this very noon hour, a girl was playing Wonder Woman with two boys. The story Mr. Bobb tells is that when he was out to get some noontime exercise, a certain girl picked two boys up and cracked their heads together like walnuts. That was his phrase, 'cracked their heads together like walnuts.' "

"She did not," I said.

"I did not," Molly told her.

"Well, that's the current story, and I suggest that if you walked in right now and spoke to Miss Hutter, she might not be at her most forgiving."

Molly leaned against the hall wall. "Well, what then?"

"Instead of sending you to the principal for punishment, I've decided that you are ripe for mediation," Miss Ivanovitch told us.

"Ripe?" Molly said.

"Mediation?" I asked.

"They want you to say you're wrong and I'm right," Nick said from the corner. "I think you should do it."

"Wait a minute," Miss Ivanovitch told us. "Everybody grab a chair and sit down in the middle of the room."

"Elevator," Nick said.

"Fair enough. In the middle of the elevator. I'll sit in your chair, Nick, in the corner, and watch what happens from here." Nick got up and moved to the middle of the elevator. She sat, and leaned forward like she was going to tell us a story. "The three of you are going to make history. Marshall and Amber just got their mediation certificates five minutes ago and you're their first conflict. But they'll do just fine. All right, each of you grab a chair."

This was going to be like a game, musical chairs, maybe. Or Sorry. She'd make us say we didn't really mean it and that would be that. We all took chairs. I set mine up across from Nick and Molly.

Amber and Marshall sat next to each other. They both looked excited and a little nervous, like it was oral report time and they were the next ones up.

"You first," Marshall whispered to her. He laid a notebook flat on his knees and unfolded a piece of paper on top of it.

"Okay." Amber glanced at her new sweatshirt, though it must have been hard to read the word "mediator" upside down. "Marshall and I are learning how to help kids solve their own problems. Do you want us to help you solve yours?"

We all looked at each other. This was weird. What could you say? I mean, you could say "no," but that would be pretty rude.

"I guess," Nick said, finally.

I shrugged.

"This is very interesting," Molly told Amber, leaning back and crossing her arms. "I bet you can't do it. Nick and Hobie want to beat each other up."

"Okay," Amber said again. "There's a way we start this whole thing off." She looked over at Miss Ivanovitch, who smiled and nodded to her. "Okay. There are four rules. One is that everything that's said here doesn't go any farther than this freight elevator. Okay?"

Everybody nodded, including Marshall.

"Okay. Rule two is that there won't be any name calling, like liar or stupid—"

"Or beet nose or prune eye?" Molly asked, grinning.

"Exactly," Amber said, seriously. "Number three, you can't interrupt when somebody else is talking. They get to finish what they have to say without anybody butting in. Okay?"

"Okay," I said.

"Four, and I guess this one is the hardest, you have to agree to tell the truth. I mean, when you tell your side of the story, you've got to try to be as honest as you can. Okay?"

She had memorized a lot of this, or at least she'd practiced it. You could tell. It was a little like being in a play, only she knew her lines and I didn't.

"Okay," I answered. "No lies." I didn't have anything to lie about.

"Okay," everybody else said. That seemed to be the one word we could all agree on.

"Marshall." Amber turned to him. "You want to take over for a while?"

I got the feeling he did. He leaned into the circle. "You're going to have to be patient with us because we've never done this before, except practicing. What we want you to do is to decide how to solve your problem. You'll tell me how, I'll write it down, and you'll sign it."

Right, I thought. Sure.

He held up the paper on his notebook. "CONTRACT" it said at the top. "So, anyway," he went on, "the first thing is for you to say what your problem is. Nick?"

Nick glanced at me and then back at Marshall. "I don't have any problem," he said, after a while.

No problem? He'd been about to beat me up. He'd pushed me down a flight of metal steps. When I tried to talk to him he stared at his stinky sneakers. But, hey, no problem. One, two, three, out go we.

"You're saying," Marshall said, "that you and Hobie have no problem?"

Nick shrugged. "Right," he said, staring past my eyes at the elevator quilt. "He's my friend."

This was dumb. This was going to be less than nothing.

Marshall turned to me. "Hobie, maybe you can tell us what your problem is."

I folded my arms and leaned back. If Molly didn't say anything, this whole thing could blow over and we'd be out of here in five minutes. "Same," I told him. "No problem. Nick's been my friend since we wore diapers."

"I hear you saying," Marshall told me, "that Nick's your friend and nothing's wrong." He glanced nervously at Miss Ivanovitch.

"Right," I told him, looking at Miss Ivanovitch, too. She did not look back. She was grading papers. I couldn't tell if she was listening or not. "Can we go now?"

Marshall turned to Molly. "And you?" he asked. "What about you? What's your problem with Nick and Hobie?"

"Oh." She opened her eyes wide with surprise. "*I* don't have any problem with them."

The bell rang. Five minutes to class time. Even in the padded elevator we could hear the yelling as the outside doors opened wide and kids hurried in from the cold.

Molly stood up. "I don't have any problem at all." She smiled. "They *both* like me."

9. I Did Not! You Did Too!

Well, that's that. Can we go now?" I asked Miss Ivanovitch.

She looked up from the papers she was grading. "What do you think, Marshall? Amber?"

"They say there isn't any problem," Marshall told her.

"But they were fighting," Amber went on. "Practically the whole fifth grade saw them fighting."

"Don't you think fighting is a problem?" Marshall asked me.

I shrugged my shoulders. Maybe if I didn't say anything, it would all go away.

Molly pulled at one of her fingers and cracked a knuckle. It sounded like when you squeeze one of those plastic bubble sheets that glass comes packed in. Everybody stared at her.

"Nick." Amber turned to him. "Can you explain why there was a fight on the playground?"

Nick kept his eyes on the floor. "Well, first off, last night Hobie got me out in the snow . . . ," he said, very quiet. His nose must have been getting better because, I noticed for the first time, he didn't sound funny anymore. "Hobie was out in the snow digging . . . something . . . up," he went on. "And then he fixed it so this wire snake hit me in the nose so it got all infected."

"I didn't mean to . . . ," I started.

"No interrupting," Amber said. "I don't understand what the snow has to do with it."

He frowned. "Nothing, I guess."

"So what you said is that Hobie hurt you with a wire snake and that your nose got red? How did that make you feel?"

Molly grinned.

"It wasn't funny," Nick told her. Then he started talking straight at me. "It made me mad. My nose hurt and it was hard to breathe, but then, to make it worse, everybody at school started laughing at me. And I guess it wasn't enough that I looked stupid and sounded weird, because then Hobie told some kids that he was going to beat me up at noon. Everybody in class, practically, was talking about how we were going to have this fight. I didn't have anything to do with it."

"Okay," Amber told him. "So you're saying that Hobie hurt you and then you heard that he was going to fight you at noon. Right?"

"Right," Nick said. "You got it."

"Hobie?" Marshall asked. "What do you think caused the fight?"

"Well, the thing is, he's only telling part of it. The snake wasn't supposed to grab his nose. It was just supposed to scare him. That's all. It wasn't my fault he jerked the wire and got it stuck. I *said* I was sorry. I think I said I was sorry. I *meant* to say I was sorry. I didn't do anything. And I didn't say I'd fight him until after these kids told me he was going to beat me up."

"Wait a minute," Molly broke in. "What wire

snake? Hobie Hanson, did you dig up our time capsule? Is that what this is all about? Was it the snake *I* buried that bit Nick? That snake was supposed to stay buried for, like, generations. You didn't!" She stood up.

I looked at the elevator floor. I thought she already knew. I thought for sure Nick had told her.

"*You're* the snake, Hobie Hanson," she said.

"Molly," Marshall told her. "You're interrupting *and* name calling. I can't believe you're doing this. That's so dumb."

We all stared at him. Something was going wrong.

"Wait a minute," Marshall said. "Play that back and erase it. Sorry."

Molly closed her mouth tight, narrowed her eyes, and popped another knuckle.

"Hobie, you're still on," Amber said.

Nick raised his hand as if we were in class. "Excuse me," he said, "but don't we have to go back now? The bell rang."

Miss Ivanovitch put the rest of her papers on the elevator floor. "Ms. O'Malley will see to it that the rest of the class gets to gym. I think this is important. Let's see what you can do. Hobie?"

110

I didn't want to miss gym. We were going to play crab soccer on floor scooters that some school had loaned us after the flood. "So," I went on, thinking and talking as fast as I could, "this morning, first thing, R.X. and Eugene came up and said Nick was out to get me because I gave him lockjaw or something, but I didn't give him anything. I knew he was mad about his nose, and I was going to talk to him about it first chance I got." I took a breath, trying to decide what to say next.

"I think what I understand," Marshall said, "is that you didn't mean to hurt Nick, that you're sorry about the snake, and that somebody told you Nick was going to beat you up."

I thought about it. So far, so good. "Right. But that's not all. See, in art class I made this really incredible clay pizza. Nick ruined it. He stepped in it. He squashed the first decent art project I've ever done in my life." I began to think what names I could call him if they'd let me call him names. I decided on some good ones. After all, that slab of clay might have won me the Grand Incredible Big Blue Ribbon in the spring art show. That pizza made real pizza look pitiful. It would have baked up all red and yellow and green and fresh-cooked brown with this glaze on it that glowed in the spotlight. "Nick Rossi," I told them, "stepped smack in the middle of my pepperoni pizza."

Molly giggled.

"It wasn't funny," I said.

Nick opened his mouth and caught his breath to say something, but Molly shook her head at him. "We promised not to interrupt," she said, and he slouched back down in his chair.

The second bell rang. Everyone was supposed to be in class. Miss Ivanovitch didn't look worried, but the bell made me talk even faster.

"The pizza smash was mean," I went on, "but then he did something even meaner. When I fell down the escalator, that wasn't any accident. Remember I had the skull part? Well, Nick shoved the leg bones and pushed me down the steps. I could have been killed. I mean, he's supposed to be my friend but he could have killed me."

I could feel my lip quiver like I was some baby, so I bit my cheeks.

Nick was staring straight at me and he was

breathing hard. If he'd been a dragon, the whole elevator would have gone up in smoke. He looked that mad.

Marshall sat quiet for a minute with his head down. When he raised it, he said, "So, what I think you said was that Nick did two things. He ruined your art project and pushed you down the escalator steps. Is that all?"

"That's plenty," I said.

Nick cleared his throat really loud.

Molly popped another knuckle.

"Excuse me, Molly," Miss Ivanovitch said. "And the rest of you. I don't mean to interrupt, but, Molly, is there some reason why you snap your knuckles like that?"

Molly held up her fingers so we could see them all. "Oh, yes. I'm doing my bone report on knuckle popping and I'm testing out the synovial fluid in my joints. There are these teeny teeny tiny bubbles in the fluid, and when the bones are pulled away from each other, like I was doing, the little bubbles form one big bubble. And when the big bubble breaks—"

"Molly," Miss Ivanovitch said, "you can give your report in class. Here we are doing something completely different."

Molly pulled the sleeves of her sweatshirt

down long so you couldn't see her hands at all. She frowned and set her teeth.

"Where were we?" Amber asked. "I guess it's your turn, Molly. All three of you were caught fighting."

"Me?" Molly asked. "You can't mean me. I don't even know why I'm here. I'm just an innocent bystander. I'm the good guy. I didn't do anything. I'm not mad at anybody, except Hobie for being a sneak and a snake, and I didn't learn that till just now. They're the ones who were mad. I *stopped* them from fighting. Remember?"

"How did you do that?" Amber asked her.

Molly let herself grin a little. She was proud of this. "I pushed them away from each other." She cocked her chin high. "I knocked them apart."

"You hit them to keep them from fighting?" Marshall asked.

"Listen," Molly said, like she was ready to pin us all to the mat, "you heard the Santa Claus person say we were getting computers because we were angels on the parking lot. Hobie and Nick would have messed things up. If I hadn't decked them, I bet there'd have been tons of blood on the snow and no new computers at Central School. They were about to prove we were no-good loser-type kids." She pushed her sweatshirt sleeves above her elbows and sat up very straight. "I did a good deed. And I'm still waiting for someone to thank me."

"Nick," Marshall said, "I think you want to say something." I'd been watching Nick, too. He'd actually been trying very hard not to butt in. I guess that's why, once he got started, the words just shot out.

"I thought you said we were supposed to tell the truth. I don't know what Hobie's talking about. First, I never told anybody I was going to beat him up. I may have said I was mad at him. I *was* mad at him, but that's all. Second . . . about the clay pepperoni pizza . . ."

You could see his eyes shift as he thought. He wasn't going to admit it. In front of all those people, he was going to lie. I could always tell when Nick was hiding something.

"I didn't do it," he said. Molly rolled her eyes. She was sitting right behind me in art class. She must have seen him smash it.

"And that's not all." He kept going. "Hobie

was practically flying down the escalator steps and I told him to slow down. He didn't, and he was running so fast I couldn't keep up, and I tripped on my shoelace. When I tripped, the skeleton fell forward. That must have pushed Hobie. But I didn't shove him. You think I'd try to murder a guy just because his lousy snake bloodied my nose? And you know what? It makes me mad he thinks I would." He really *was* mad. "Who does he think I am?"

"Hobie?" Amber looked at me.

"You tripped?" I asked him.

"I tripped."

This time he didn't look like he was lying. Maybe it was possible that he tripped on the escalator. Maybe I *was* rushing too fast. Maybe. "You didn't push me?"

"I didn't mean to push you."

"They said you said you were going to beat me up," I told him.

"They lied," he said. "Did you tell them you were going to double my nose at noon?"

"No," I told him. "I never did. Everybody was waiting for us to fight, though. Everybody expected it. *Somebody* must have said it."

"Then I think you're agreeing," Amber said

116

slowly, "that, even though you were mad at each other, you didn't fight because you wanted to, but because other kids told you to. Is that right?"

"I guess," I said.

"Looks like it," Nick told her. "And I didn't mean to hurt him."

"Neither me," I said.

"So, that takes care of the past," Marshall said. "What about the future?"

"The future?" Nick and I said at the same time.

"I mean, what if some kid comes up and tells you how he's heard you're going to bounce each other off the walls of the boys' washroom tomorrow? Does that mean you'll do it?" He held up the paper that had "CONTRACT" written at the top.

I saw Miss Ivanovitch sneak a look at her watch.

"You want us to say we'll never argue? Is that it?" Nick asked him.

"That'd be dumb," Molly said.

"She's right," I told Marshall. "That'd be really stupid."

"Okay, what *can* you agree to?" Amber asked.

"I don't know," Nick said. "To talk to Hobie when I'm mad at him, I guess, instead of just getting madder and madder."

Marshall wrote something on the paper. "Hobie?" he asked me.

"Same, I guess. Not fight just because R.X. and Eugene tell me to. I guess I could say I'm sorry I did the stuff I did even though it wasn't on purpose."

"What about the time capsule?" Molly asked. "I mean, *I'm* mad about that."

"I was going to put that back, anyway," I told her. "Okay, you can write down that I'll bury the time capsule again tonight."

"And not dig it up again, but wait for somebody else to do it like they're supposed to in 2013," Molly said.

"You can add that," I told Marshall, who was getting it all down.

"Molly," Marshall said, "I've got your name, too. So, what should I say? Molly Bosco agrees to . . ."

"I didn't do anything wrong," she said. There was this long silence. "Well," she told Marshall, "if you think there's such a big problem, *you* can solve it."

"That's not the point," he said. "I'm supposed to help you think of a way to solve it."

Molly sighed loudly.

Miss Ivanovitch stood up. "The class is going to be back very soon from gym. I'm afraid I must leave. You're all doing a fine job. Molly, I'm confident you'll think of something. After you've come to an agreement, just sign the contract and get back to class as soon as you can." Clutching her stack of papers and books, she hurried out of the elevator and down the dark hall.

We all watched as she dropped a couple of papers, stopped to grab them up, and then, with her shoulder, pushed open the big swinging door that led from the back hall into the school. When the door swung shut, we all looked at Molly.

"All right, all right," she said, sighing again to let us know she didn't want to do what she was doing. "I'll agree to something. I'll agree to let Nick and Hobie beat each other up if they want to. How's that?"

Marshall wrote something down. Then he read out loud what was on the page.

C O N T R A C T

PROBLEM <u>fighting on the playground</u>

The people whose signatures appear below, with the help of two media-tors, have reached the following agreement:

<u>Hobie Hanson</u> agrees
- <u>not to fight Nick just because someone tells him to.</u>
- <u>to say he's sorry he hurt Nick's nose.</u>
- <u>to bury the time capsule tonight and not dig it up until the year 2013.</u>
<u>Nick Rossi</u> agrees
- <u>to try talk to Hobie when he's mad at him.</u>
- <u>to say he's sorry Hobie fell down the escalator.</u>
- <u>not to fight Hobie because other kids say to.</u>
<u>Molly Bosco agrees</u>
- <u>to stay out of Nick and Hobie's arguments</u>

We have made and signed this con-tract because we believe it solves our problem. We will hold to it.

_____   _____

_____

Mediators <u>Marshall Ezry</u>
          <u>Amber Murnyak</u>

"That's not exactly what I said," Molly told him, but when it came her turn, she signed anyway.

"Congratulations," Amber told us. "That was great. I mean, you just . . ."

"This elevator's driving me bananas," Nick said, folding up his chair and leaning it against the quilted wall. "I keep thinking it's going to move." Then he lowered his voice so only I could hear it. "I'm sorry you fell," he said. "I really am."

"I know," I said, leaning my chair next to his. "Me, too, about your nose. What do you say we push button number two, ride up to the second floor, and then walk down the escalator?" I turned around and faced the control panel. "Or would you rather go to the basement?"

"I think you're in enough trouble already," Molly said.

Nick grinned. "Go ahead. Push it," he said. "We can always say we fell against it in a fight."

Amber and Marshall didn't laugh. I decided not to wait for their votes. I just put my thumb over the button marked two and pushed.

The elevator didn't go up. It didn't go down either. It sat there like an ordinary room.

Something did happen, though. It was like he appeared because I pushed the button. Standing square in front of the elevator door, his hands on his belly, with a frown you never see in pictures, was my old friend Santa Claus.

10. Not What They Used to Be

Ho, Santa Claus," I called. Maybe the elevator doors would zap shut and disappear us. I waited. We stayed put and he stayed put, so I kept talking. "So, how's the weather at the North Pole annex? And how's your funny nephew, Oscar Claus?"

He did not smile. Lines deepened on his forehead. "What's going on here?" he asked, peering into the corners behind us. "Where is your teacher?"

"Miss Ivanovitch just went back to class, Mr. Claus," Molly said sweetly, stepping out of the elevator as if it was Cinderella's coach. She knew this was the guy who'd announced the computer gifts. "We're on our way there right now, if you'd like to see her."

"You're unsupervised," he said.

"We're trusted, sir," Marshall told him. "We've just finished mediating a dispute." He pointed to his sweatshirt.

"But these young people were fighting on the playground," Santa Claus said. "With my own eyes I saw you, you, and you." He pointed to Nick, Molly, and me.

"Ah," Nick said, figuring out who he was, "and I saw you, too."

"They worked it out," Amber explained.

"You've heard of the Mayflower Compact?" I asked him. "Well, we just signed the Freight Elevator Compact." I hoped that would make us sound as good as pilgrim kids in the *really* old days.

"We helped them make an agreement," Marshall said, holding up the signed paper.

"Oh? Not to fight again?" Santa asked.

"Not exactly," I told him.

He shook his head. "Before this noon I'd assumed this was a group of *good* boys and girls. That's why I'd planned to reward you."

"We still get our computers, don't we?" Molly

asked. "I mean, Nick and Hobie didn't actually fight. Nobody got blood on the snow."

"You have to earn rewards," Santa Claus told her, without saying yes or no.

"Oscar argues all the time. Where is he?" I asked. Maybe the puppet could make him laugh.

"I put Oscar away, tucked him in my pocket. I've decided I don't need him anymore," Santa Claus said. He was beginning to sound more sad than mad.

"We better get back," Marshall said, and he and Amber headed toward the swinging door that led to the floor of classes.

"Of course you should," Santa Claus said, waving us off. "And so should I. Be on your way."

"Why don't you need Oscar?" Molly asked, stopping in front of him, blocking his way. "I thought Oscar was kind of funny. Did he ever hear the joke about what kind of dog has no tail?" She sounded nice, actually, and hardly bratty at all. It was pretty clear we were dealing here with one gloomy Santa Claus.

"We'll tell Miss Ivanovitch you're coming," Amber called as the door swung shut.

"Did Oscar lose his voice?" Nick tried.

"Is it because *he*'s always fighting?" I asked. I mean, that would be pretty bizarre, since he and Oscar were the same guy. But Oscar *was* always butting in.

He looked at me funny. "No, though I guess he is at that." He pulled off his stocking cap and curly white wig. The fringe of hair around his bald spot was damp. "Maybe I haven't kept up with the times, but the more I listened to all of those boys and girls in the igloo this morning, the more I realized that children just aren't what they used to be." He shook his head. "I can't go on with it."

"Can't go on with what?" Nick asked him.

"What did they used to be?" I asked. I'd always wondered. I wasn't around in the old days. "Were kids smarter? Quieter? Like, seen but not heard?" I asked him.

"I bet you quit your job," Molly said. "Is that why you don't need Oscar anymore?"

He tucked his head like he was embarrassed. "Well, I suited up for this afternoon, but when this shift's over . . ." He unhooked the beard that was strapped to his head, pulled it off, and stuffed it and the wig inside his red cap.

126

Molly caught her breath. "Wait a minute. You're Mr. Bobb!" she said. "I didn't know that. You know what? You look really good in a beard. Have you ever thought about growing one?"

"You young people had better go back to class," he told us.

"Okay," I said, "but first tell us why you quit." It didn't matter if we were a little late. Nobody was going to throw us out of school for cheering up Kris Kringle. The kids would hardly be back from gym. We started walking slowly down the hall.

He shook his head. "I thought I'd enjoy playing Santa Claus. I thought I'd bounce little children on my knee and they'd tell me they wanted sleds and lollipops and rubber dollies that cry and wet and say 'Ma-Ma.' "

"And it wasn't like that?" Nick asked him.

"Most of them seemed afraid of me. One of them pulled Oscar right off my hand. And all of them had lists of very strange presents."

"Like what?" I asked him, though I had a pretty good idea.

"Plastic toys, mostly. Television toys. They wanted me to slide down their chimneys," he said, "with guns called Laser Dazers that stun space aliens, and they asked for small creatures with odd names who, I gather, live in sewers." He shook his head. "Children are *not* what they used to be."

"I bet you had a BB gun when you were little and played Cowboys and Indians," Molly said.

He grinned. "I did. You're right. I did."

"That's disgusting," Molly told him. "You could really hurt somebody with a BB gun, and Indians were the fathers of our country. And the mothers."

"We better get back, no joke," I said. She was starting to say all the wrong things again. Our computers were disappearing in a puff of smoke. We all began to walk faster toward the swinging door.

"You may have something there," Santa told Molly. "You're a smart girl. You may have something there." He stopped walking. "But we didn't play with *slime.* A little girl in a fluorescent frock, which her mother had *not* bought at Bob's Togs, asked me to bring her slime—a bucket, she said, of slime. Do you think she might have had a lisp?"

I stepped behind Santa Claus and motioned for Molly to say yes.

"Did she want anything else?" Molly asked him.

He frowned as though he was trying to remember. "She asked for a scuba Barbie, a live hamster, and slime."

We started moving on again.

"I thought at first," he went on, "that she might have said 'sublime,' but she was a little young to know the word *sublime*."

"How about something to climb?" Molly was thinking fast. "Good children like to climb. Maybe that was it."

"No." He shook his head. "You don't have buckets of something to climb."

As we pushed the door open and left the back hall for the school, you could hear the classes going full blast. In one space some kids were doing their Thanksgiving skit with the papier-mâché turkey I'd seen that morning. We walked past Ms. O'Malley's class. Two guys were standing in front next to Mort the skeleton. His arm was still slung in Miss Ivanovitch's scarf. The guys were singing the "leg bone's connected to the hip bone" song, probably giving a joint report. A few kids waved at us and pointed at Santa Claus holding his hair.

In Mr. Star's class, everybody was breaking up at one of his jokes. You could tell it was Mr. Star's joke because he was laughing loudest.

Our beardless, wigless Santa Claus blinked at the noise. "My store was never this loud," he said.

"Maybe that's what was wrong with it," Molly told him. If she kept this up, he was going to make us give *him* computers.

Miss Ivanovitch peered around the chalkboard that was at the front of our class. She waved at us.

"Better put your disguise back on," I told Mr. Bobb. "Think of all the kids you'll shock if you don't."

I think I saw him roll his eyes. But he hooked the beard over his head and plopped the wig on top. The cap, though, stayed in his pocket with Oscar.

"Well, hello there, Santa," Miss Ivanovitch said as Molly guided him into our room. "The snow outside must make you feel right at home." She turned and held her finger to her lips to shush the kids who were starting to laugh at him.

Laughing at him was probably not a smart

move. They didn't know they weren't this guy's idea of perfect. I bet even Miss Ivanovitch wasn't his idea of perfect. I bet he never had a teacher like her in the old days. I headed back to my seat, trying to think of some way to warn them all not to say totally the wrong things.

"Miss Ivanovitch," Molly explained, "this may look like Santa Claus, but he's really Mr. Bobb, the genuine Mr. Robert 'Bob' Bobb."

"Some of us had guessed," Miss Ivanovitch said, as she reached out and shook his hand with both of hers. He smiled and nodded to the group the way a proper Santa would.

"Nice to see you all, but I really must be going," he said politely, adding a weak, "Ho-ho-ho."

Molly held him firmly by the elbow. "Miss Ivanovitch," she said, "Mr. Bobb caught us in the elevator and he thought we were breaking rules or something. Would you please tell him what we were doing was okay?"

"I don't know," Miss Ivanovitch said. "Was what you were doing okay?" She looked at Molly like she couldn't be quite sure.

"What *were* you doing?" Lisa asked, giggling.

Nick sank down in his seat. "Of course it was okay," he told Miss Ivanovitch. "We signed this contract about fighting. *We're* okay. If you want to know the truth, it's Mr. Bobb who's got the problem. He's about to quit his Santa Claus job."

"He keeps saying kids aren't what they used to be," I told her.

"Oh, I know exactly what you mean," she told Mr. Bobb. "The world is different, even from when I was little." Nick, Molly, and I all groaned at once. Whose side was she on, anyway?

R.X. raised his hand. "My grandfather is always telling my sister and me that kids used to be more polite," R.X. said. "But my grandmother told us that when he was ten years old he turned over an outhouse on Halloween. That doesn't sound polite to me."

Santa Bob chuckled. He didn't laugh. He didn't giggle. He chuckled, like Santa Claus would. "But that was good old-fashioned fun," he said.

"I wouldn't do it. I think it's gross," R.X. told him. "Maybe kids *are* different."

This was not going well. This was not going well at all.

"That's not what I meant," Santa said.

"Sit down, Mr. Bobb." Miss Ivanovitch pulled her chair out for him and he sat. "We'd love to talk to Santa Claus."

He leaned forward, his arms on the desk. He was staring up at a sign that still hung high on the far wall. "Bob's Best Bargains," it said. "What I meant," he explained, "was . . . well, among other things, in my day school wasn't like this." He shook his finger at us as if we'd been bad, or maybe naughty.

"In my day," he went on, "school was silent. Students didn't sing to skeletons. They didn't *need* computers. They wrote their essays in ink and did their arithmetic with good old-fashioned pencil and paper. When children had fights they were disciplined by the proper authorities. And when they played, they played with good old-fashioned toys."

Santa Bobb stood up, pulled his cap out of his pocket, and plopped it on top of his head. As he did, Oscar, the puppet, dropped to the floor, grinning. Santa stared down at it.

"I remember," the puppet on the floor said sadly, "the good old days when kids were called children."

11. The Santa Clause

Marshall stood up. "Mr. Bobb," he said, "Amber and I have just finished this class in how to mediate arguments. Miss Ivanovitch and some lawyers came in and talked to us every lunchtime for weeks. So far we've only done it once—in the elevator with Nick and Hobie and Molly—and we're not sure if that took or not." He reached down, picked up Oscar, and handed him to Mr. Bobb. "But what I wondered was, what if we tried it between you and . . ." He looked around, trying to think of a word.

"Kids," Molly filled in the blank. "Between you and kids."

Mr. Bobb frowned and shook his head. "I'm

sorry," he told Marshall and Molly, "but I feel certain there is a long line of them waiting for me outside the igloo. The sign says I'm feeding my reindeer, and that I will be back"—he looked at his watch—"ten minutes from right now."

"Oh, but it seems like a wonderful opportunity," Miss Ivanovitch told him. "We'll only take ten minutes. Do stay."

"Well . . . ," he said.

"I'm afraid the first question may be the hardest, though," she went on. "It's . . ." She nodded to Amber.

"Do you agree to solve the problem?" Amber asked him.

He shook his head. "That's why this is really unnecessary," he said. "There is no problem." I almost laughed, because that's exactly what Nick had said at first. That's what I had said, too, and Molly. He put the puppet on his hand like it was a mitten and he was about to go out into the cold.

"Well, *we* have a problem," I said, from the back of the class. "You called us names and we're mad."

"Name calling is one of those things you've

got to agree not to do in mediation," Amber told him.

His face got red enough to match the pink makeup on his cheeks. He looked set to explode.

"You do seem to be angry with us," Amber said. "Sit down and we'll try. Please."

He cocked his head to the side and the anger began to slide off his face. "I like the word 'please,' " he said. "It's one word that's been lost by this generation. That and 'thank you.' "

Nobody said anything.

Santa Bobb looked around the room and sat down on the edge of Miss Ivanovitch's chair, as if he might pop up and away at any minute.

Marshall held up a sheet of paper. "This is a contract form, and I have to write some names down on it, but I don't know what to write. Do I call you Robert 'Bob' Bobb or Santa Claus?"

"One and the same."

"Not exactly," Marshall told him.

"All right," he said, sounding pretty impatient. "Write down Robert Bobb."

"But we have to talk to Santa, too," I said.

"He's the one who's going to face off against those innocent kids this afternoon."

"Not so innocent." Santa crossed his arms and leaned back. "I know what they see on television."

Around the room people were beginning to talk to each other, trying to find out from Nick and Molly and Amber what this was all about and passing it on. The sound level rose. Miss Ivanovitch held out her hands and stopped it.

"Mr. Bobb has a point," she said. "Some of you may have forgotten that politeness is a virtue."

We shut our mouths.

"If you don't mind, Mr. Bobb, perhaps we *could* talk with Santa, too," Miss Ivanovitch said, and she grinned. "That way we could put a special section in the contract—a separate clause just for him."

Nick got it first: "A *Santa* clause!"

Mr. Bobb laughed out loud. That was something Oscar might have said.

"All right," he told Miss Ivanovitch. "I'll listen."

"I'm afraid you'll have to do more than listen," Amber explained. "You'll have to talk." She turned to Miss Ivanovitch. "Can we really do this? I'm not sure. I mean, who talks for the other side?"

Molly raised her hand. "I'll do it. I'm a typical kid," she said.

Nick groaned at that and raised his hand.

So did I.

Lisa flung her arm around like she was trying to get rid of it. Pretty soon everybody's arm was up.

"We're wasting time," Mr. Bobb said, checking his watch.

"I've got an idea," Amber told us. "Anybody can talk because we're all kids, but we can't interrupt each other because *not* interrupting is part of the rules. So, what if Mr. Bobb calls on the one he wants to hear. Okay?"

Mr. Bobb looked over the room. A few hands were already up. He nodded to Marshall.

"I think," Marshall said, "you've already pretty much told us your problem. You think that children aren't as good as they used to be because they're louder in school, they aren't polite, and they use computers instead of pencils and pens. Is that all?"

Mr. Bobb thought about it. "Also," he said, "in my day, teachers were in charge of settling arguments." He raised his chin high and the white beard stuck out above his coat so you could really see it was fake.

"I hear you saying," Marshall added, "you think we shouldn't learn how to settle our own arguments."

"Did I say that?" Mr. Bobb asked. "I'm not sure I meant that. But let it be." He pointed to my raised hand.

"*Our* problem," I told him, "is that we don't think it's fair that you don't like us just because we're not like you were when you were our age. But I bet they didn't have TV when you were our age, or computers. How do you know what you would have been like if they did?"

"So what Hobie is saying," Marshall decided, "is that times are different and he doesn't like being blamed for it."

"Right," I told them, "right." A lot of kids agreed.

"What can you do to resolve this problem?" Amber said.

Mr. Bobb blinked, like he had no idea.

"Have you ever used a computer?" R.X. asked. R.X. is like a real computer whiz. "I mean, I bet you haven't," he said, "because if you had, you'd know a computer doesn't write for you or do your math. You've got to know what you're doing to use one."

"No, I never needed—" Mr. Bobb started.

"Well, what we could do is show you how. That might solve part of the problem." What R.X. meant is that *he* could show him how. Except Mr. Bobb would sit down with R.X. and feel like a dope in about two seconds, R.X. knows so much. That might just make him madder. "You'll need to use computers in your new store. You're going to start a new store, aren't you?"

"Well, I . . ."

Eugene's hand went up. Mr. Bobb nodded at him like he was glad to leave R.X. behind.

"How about selling beds this time?" Eugene suggested. "Bob's Beds? You could have them shaped like sneakers and race cars and candy bars and . . ."

"And books with sheets of paper," Mr. Bobb added, laughing. "You're ganging up on me. If I stay much longer you might convince me you're alright. But I *must* go." He stood up.

"Wait," Marshall told him. "Please. I want to do the Santa clause."

"No need," Mr. Bobb said, "I won't be Santa much longer. There are just too many children wanting too many toys I've never heard of." Nick raised his hand. Mr. Bobb kept talking as though he knew what Nick was going to say. "I suppose I *could* try to—"

Lisa, who'd had her hand up for a long time, just started talking. "I wouldn't worry about it if I were you. You're not going to have, like, that many kids anymore. Starting this afternoon—I heard this on the radio yesterday—they're going to make valuable keepsake video recordings of all visits to Santa Claus at the Old Oak Mall. And that's only about a mile from here. Nobody will be coming to the Wilhurst Mall to see you."

Santa Claus's furry white jaw dropped. You could tell this was news to him.

"So they'll just stop coming," Lisa went on. "All those screaming children. It's, like, no big deal."

"They didn't scream," he said. He looked disappointed. His shoulders slumped. Then his puppet hand came up.

"Let's just chuck the whole thing, Unc," Oscar said. "There's probably no one out there, anyway."

Nick got up from his desk, slipped a yellow construction-paper bathroom pass to Miss

Ivanovitch, mumbled something to her, and fled. I wondered if his beet nose had suddenly turned into lockjaw.

Lisa flung her arm up again and kept it up as she talked. "I heard that about the videos on WOGR radio," she said, "so I know it's true. And if parents or guardians don't want to, like, buy the precious video keepsake, they still get a complete computer printout of that once-in-a-lifetime conversation, so they'll know what cute things their kid said and what he or she wants most in the whole wide world."

"We didn't do anything like that here," Santa said. "All we have in the igloo is me and my old friend." He held up Oscar, who shook his red head sadly, like he couldn't think of a single funny thing to say.

"May I have your attention please," an out-of-breath voice announced. It bounced across the ceiling of our Bob's Togs school. "Santa Claus is needed in the mall." The phony low voice *could* have been calling from just about anywhere, but I knew exactly where it was. It was coming from the spy place that Nick had found the first day we were in the mall. It came from the room where Mr. Bobb had been resting when he saw me fall down the escalator. I didn't look toward the vent where I knew Nick was standing, his hands cupped around his mouth.

"The children in the mall," the voice went on, "need to talk to Santa Claus in his igloo." It was Nick. If Miss Hutter caught him, he'd had it.

Santa Claus didn't seem to wonder who it was. He'd been called. He straightened his shoulders and then bowed slightly to Miss Ivanovitch.

"This has been most instructional," he told her, "but I really must be going."

"Just a second," Molly said, as he started away. "Mr. Santa Claus Bobb, do we get the computers even though we're not perfect?"

He looked shocked that she'd asked.

"Your principal said you need them," he told her. "I'm a man of my word."

Molly smiled. "Thank you," she said.

"Please come to see us anytime," Miss Ivanovitch called to him.

He waved his Oscar hand. "I will," he said. "I expect I will."

Whenever you walk through the school door into the mall, a laser beam triggers a bell. It's to announce people coming in and to catch kids sneaking out. Just as Nick slid back into his front row seat again, the laser-beam bell went *bong.* Santa Claus was on his way out to more TV kids wanting more Grape Goop and Action Video Vampires. He'd never last.

12. Onward!

Toooobbbby," the little girl yelled. "You go get it. You're a big booger. You get my Snow-baller. Right now."

Nick, Molly, and I had gone straight to my house after school. We were in my backyard to bury the time capsule for the last time. This little girl from Toby's nursery school was playing with him—actually she was fighting with him—till her mother got out of work.

"Get her toy," Nick told Toby. The little girl had been shoveling snow into a purple plastic mold. The thing was supposed to form perfect snowballs. Toby had heaved it from my yard to his, right over the fence.

"Toooooby," she yelled again. She looked like

she was going to cry us a flood of tears. The snowstorm, though, was over, and the late-afternoon sun was shining pink through the clouds. It made the ground look like cotton candy.

"I won't," Toby said. "She called me a big booger."

"I want my Snowballer," she said, and she began to cry.

"You're a baby," Toby said. "Big kids make snowballs with their hands."

"I'm not a baby," the girl told him.

"You've got a Snowballer. That makes you a baby. Lakeesha is a baby," he sang.

Lakeesha hit him with her plastic shovel.

"Cut it out," Nick told them.

"Toby's a big, big, *big* booger," she said, and she hit him again, harder. Now they were both crying.

"Shut up," I yelled.

A lot of good that did.

"Wait a minute," Molly said. She sat in a mound of snow and pulled them down with her.

"All right now, will you both agree to tell me the truth?"

"Huh?" Toby asked.

"I'm not a baby," Lakeesha said.

"Will you agree not to interrupt when the other kid is talking?" Molly went on.

"I want to go home," Lakeesha said, digging a cave with her shovel.

"You're supposed to make snowballs with your hands," Toby said.

"Okay," Molly told them, "let's try it this way. Lakeesha, what's the matter?"

"I want my Snowballer. It's mine. My daddy gave it to me. Snow makes my hands cold." Her nose was running but she didn't seem to notice. Maybe it would freeze into stalactites.

"Okay," Molly said again. "It's your turn, Toby. "What's the matter?"

Toby stuck out his bottom lip. "I'm not a booger. Besides, she won't let me use her Snowballer."

"But I thought you said only ba—" I started, but Molly gave me a look that would stop a truck.

"Okay, Lakeesha," Molly went on, "what can you do to solve this problem?"

Lakeesha sniffed. "If he gets it, he can make two snowballs," she said.

"How does that sound to you?" Molly asked

Toby. "You go get the toy and Lakeesha will let you use it twice to see how it works."

"She called me a booger," he said.

"You didn't like that?"

"It stunk."

"You called *me* a baby. That stunk like a skunk."

Toby wrinkled his nose.

"What can you do about that?" Molly asked him.

"I won't call her a baby if she won't call me a booger."

"Okay? Okay. Well, then, that's settled," Molly said, standing up. "I'm a pro at this. Scoot," she told Toby, and he headed off toward his yard.

I turned back to my mound of snow. Only a few more scoops and the time hole would be completely uncovered. I'd thought the dirt would be frozen stiff by now, but the snow blanket had kept it soft.

"Hurry back, Toby, we're going to bury the time capsule again. Now," I explained to Nick and Molly, "I've got all the original stuff here, ready to go—including the fake peanut brittle can."

"I object," Nick said, pulling his plaid scarf up to his eyes. "Somebody in the far future is going to get hurt."

"That was a chance in a million," Molly told him. "Nobody, *nobody* else would ever get that snake hooked in his nose. But if he did, everybody would laugh. Your nose, by the way, looks much better. Like a *small* beet."

Nick tried not to smile. "I still don't see what was so funny." He did, though, I know he did.

"But your eye . . ." Molly turned to me. "Your eye is going to be much worse tomorrow." She was right. I could feel it turning fatter and purpler.

Toby slogged back through the snowbanks and dropped the snowball maker at Lakeesha's feet. "You can have it. I don't want it."

Neither did Lakeesha. They left it in the snow and stamped over to stare in my fresh, deep hole. I picked up the coffee can filled with my baby teeth, glow-in-the-dark shoelaces, and other Future Stunners. I'd taped the can round and round and round to make it flood proof and gopher proof. Then I placed it in the cracker tin and fastened the lid tight. Molly held out one of the big plastic garbage bags, and I dropped the whole capsule inside.

"Onward to the year 2013!" I held the bag high.

"Onward!" Molly said, shaking her fist like we were troops.

We both looked at Nick. "Onward," he mumbled.

"Hey, I got something else for onward," Toby said.

"What you got?" Nick asked him.

"It's this thing I made in nursery school." He reached in his pocket and pulled out a triangle wrapped in foil.

"Oh, I did one of those," Lakeesha said.

"Whatever it is, it's too big," I told him. "Besides, the can's already taped up."

"Can't I just stick it in the bag? Can't I?" He peeled off the foil and showed us what was inside. "Maybe those people won't know what pizza is."

What he was holding wasn't a wedge of real pizza, of course. It was made out of clay, the plastic clay little kids use that already has color in it. It wasn't real earth clay like I'd used to make my practically perfect pepperoni pizza that morning.

I looked at Nick. He looked at the sky.

"How come you made pizza?" I asked Toby.

"I don't know."

"We all did," Lakeesha told me.

"Mine was best," Toby said.

"It looks disgusting," I told him.

"It looks delicious," Molly said, patting him on the head like he was a good puppy and giving me this look like I should be ashamed of myself for talking mean to such an adorable little boy.

I didn't want Molly to mediate a fight between me and a four-year-old kid. "What's your pizza got on it?" I asked him, being Mr. Nice Guy.

"Worms," he said, "and"—he smiled—"toe jam."

Lakeesha giggled like this was the joke of the century.

Nick groaned.

Molly rolled her eyes.

"All right," I told him. "I don't know if the future is ready for toe jam and worm pizza, but we'll let them decide."

He squashed the foil around the clay and dropped the silver package into the bag. It clunked against the coffee can.

"I might have put my art project in, too, but

your brother stepped in it," I told him, just to let Nick know I hadn't forgotten.

"No he didn't," Molly said.

"He did so," I told her. "He even said he was sorry. In the freight elevator. Remember?"

Nick raised his scarf higher. He looked like a bandit. "I said I was sorry you came back and found it like that."

"Same difference," I told him, trying to catch his eye to see if he really was sorry. Both his eyes were practically hidden by the scarf.

"He didn't smash it," Molly said, walking in a circle, making footprints in the snow.

"Who did, then?"

She looked at me and grinned. "Nobody."

"Somebody had to. It was smashed."

"No it wasn't."

"I saw it with my own eyes. That clay looked like an elephant had tap-danced on it."

"That was not an elephant foot," Molly said. "That was my foot, but it wasn't your pizza. When you were up talking to Mr. Sciarra, I just rolled out a quick slice of clay and jumped on it. You never like the art stuff you do, so I thought you'd think it was funny. Anyway, I got my sneaker all yucky."

"Is that true?" I asked Nick.

He nodded.

"Why didn't you tell me?"

"He was being a gentleman," Molly said. "*Some* people know how to be gentlemen."

I thought about hitting her. I really thought about it.

"But then," she went on, "after you and Nick left to get the skeleton, I took your real piece of pizza up and gave it to Mr. Sciarra. I told him that the one with lots of states of Texas on it was what you'd actually made. I told him the first one was just a joke."

"What did he say?" I asked her. "What did he say about my art project?"

"He said," Molly told me, "that it was very interesting. Actually, I think he liked the first one better."

"I would have told you," Nick said, "sooner or later. The freight elevator didn't seem the best time or place."

Molly smiled at him like she thought he was wonderful. And I didn't care. It didn't matter to me who she liked. I didn't like her.

I just shrugged my shoulders and tied a knot in the garbage bag. Then I put it in another garbage bag and tied an even tighter knot in that one. Then I tucked it into the hole. We all took turns covering the bags with dirt— even Nick and Lakeesha, who hadn't been there last summer when the time capsule was buried.

"What I want to know," I asked Nick, "is why you didn't have to stay after school."

"After school?" Molly asked.

"After school?" Nick echoed her.

"The voice from the wall," I said, "the one that told Santa the kids wanted him, wasn't that you?"

"It didn't *sound* like you," Molly said.

Nick shrugged. "If it was, they didn't catch me."

"If they'd caught you, I predict that it wouldn't have gone to the mediators," I told him.

"If Miss Hutter had caught you up there, she'd have called your parents and you'd be grounded for life—or at least a week." Molly stared at him to see if she could tell if he did it.

"Who said it was me?" Nick asked in that phony low voice that had made the announcement. "Anyway, some crimes are never ever punished."

It was darker now and the snow wasn't pink anymore. Toby and Lakeesha were jumping up and down on the dirty mound like it was a trampoline.

"Guess what?" Toby said when he stopped jumping.

"What?" Molly asked him.

"*That*'s what!" He laughed and laughed like he'd really got us. "Guess what else."

Nick lowered his scarf. "Don't ask him," he told Molly. "He'll keep it up for hours."

"Guess what else." Toby tried again.

"What else?" I said.

"I saw Santa Claus today."

Nick and Molly and I looked at each other.

"How?" Nick asked him.

"Mom took me after nursery school."

"Where?"

"She took me, too," Lakeesha said. "It was in that place."

"What place?" Molly was getting annoyed.

"That place you go to school," Toby explained. "That mall. They've got an igloo in the middle of it. Did you know that? It's not cold inside, but it's a real igloo. Santa Claus was there."

"Did you talk to him?" I couldn't wait to

hear. "What did you tell him you wanted for Christmas?"

"You didn't say you wanted a Laser Dazer, did you?" Molly asked him.

He shook his head.

What was worse than a space gun? "A wind-up cockroach?" I tried.

He shook his head again, grinning. How bad could it be?

"Slime?" Nick asked. Couldn't get much worse than that.

Toby waited, like he was going to say yes, but then he shook his head back and forth and back and forth. "No, no, no." He clamped his lips tight, crossed his arms, and shut us out.

Molly took a nickel out of her pocket, held it up so he could see, and then dropped it down the neck of his jacket.

He shivered from the cold of the coin against his skin, but it started his voice box. "Santa Claus said I could ask for three things. I told him I wanted a little red car, the kind you can park under your pillow at night and it won't keep you awake. That was one. Then I told him I wanted a wood sled."

"A little red car and a wooden sled?" Molly

turned to us. "Why would he lie about that? It has to be true. But that's perfect. That's like he's the old-fashioned child Mr. Bobb thought had disappeared with the dinosaurs."

Nick, I could tell, didn't believe in Toby as the perfect small person. "But you've *got* a sled," Nick told him. "Why would you ask for a new sled?"

Toby sat down on the snow mound and spun himself around. When he stopped he said, "My dumb plastic saucer cracked in half. It's junk. I want a sled that'll last. I told Santa Claus that."

Nick's jaw hung open.

"What else?" I asked him. "That's only two."

"World peace," he said.

World peace? All three of us gasped together.

"Did you say world peace?" Nick stuck his face up close to Toby's like he was trying to read it.

"We talked about that in nursery school today," Lakeesha said. "It means everybody is nice to everybody else. That's good."

"Santa Claus smiled," Toby told us, "and then he took a fuzzy puppet out of his pocket. The puppet's name was Oscar."

That was our Santa Claus all right.

"He said,"—and the kid beamed—"he said I was a *good* boy."

"A good boy?" Nick shook his head. "Good? You? He should have talked to me first."

"What did *you* say?" Molly asked.

This time Toby grinned, a sly grin like he knew he'd told Santa Claus something that was absolutely right.

"I said 'Thank you,' and Santa Claus laughed like maybe he'd bring me something even better than what I asked for."

"Tell them what you *did*," Lakeesha said, giggling.

Toby's face fell. He looked around at all of us like maybe this wasn't as good as the rest.

"If you don't tell, I will," Lakeesha said.

Toby grabbed onto the loose tail of Nick's scarf and rubbed it against his face. Then he stuck his thumb in his mouth.

"You did everything else right. It can't be all that bad," Molly told him. "What did you do?"

He pulled his thumb out, and looking at his toes, he said, "I got so excited, I peed on his knee."

"You what?" Nick asked.

It wasn't possible. He was making it up. "Not

on Santa Claus's knee," I said. "This was later, right? Somewhere else."

"On Santa Claus's knee," Lakeesha said. "Right there."

Nick looked like he was going to pick Toby up and toss him over the fence.

"Okay, you peed on his knee," Molly said. "I bet you had on waterproof snowpants."

Toby shook his head and stuck out his bottom lip.

Molly took a deep breath. "No joke?"

"No joke," Lakeesha said. "I was there."

"Was Santa Claus mad?" I asked. What did I mean, was he mad? Of course he was mad.

Toby giggled. "Guess what Oscar said. He said, 'The boys' washroom is on the second floor, not the second knee.' He had this funny Smurfy voice."

"Toby cried," Lakeesha said.

"I did not. Only a little bit. And then Santa Claus picked me up and put me on the step in front of his chair. First he looked at the wet place. Then he looked at the puppet and he said, 'Oscar, I think we kept him waiting in line too long.' "

"That's when Toby stopped crying," Lakeesha said.

160

Toby wiped his nose on his sleeve and climbed to the top of the time machine hill. "Guess what," he asked.

"What?" I asked him back.

"That's what," he said, without skipping a beat. "Guess what else. Oscar asked me to come back some day and I said I would. I said I'd bring my whole nursery school with me. And guess what Santa Claus said."

"I can't imagine," I told him.

"He didn't *say* anything." Toby giggled. "He gave me a red and green candy cane. Oscar said something. Oscar looked right at me and he said, 'You know what, Santa Claus? Kids *will* be kids.' "

Jamie Gilson is the author of ten popular books for children. She has won numerous Best Book awards voted by the readers themselves.

Ms. Gilson loves to talk with young people and travels often to speak in schools and libraries. Many of her story ideas are based on what her audiences tell her. There really is a school that was flooded and had to set up temporary classrooms in a shopping mall. And today's students really are learning to resolve their own problems and disputes through mediation.

She and her husband, a lawyer, live in a suburb of Chicago, Illinois. Mort also lives in Illinois.